CEO GROUPIE

by

M.H. VESSEUR

CEO GROUPIE

A RADIO DETECTIVE

A novel by

M.H. VESSEUR

Vibes Publishing

Published by Vibes

www.mhvesseur.com

www.facebook.com/MHVesseur

Second edition

ISBN 978-94-91908-40-8 (paperback, 2nd edition)

ISBN 978-90-806920-0-8 (epub with DRM for Amazon Kindle)

CEO Groupie

One

The opening tune blazed onto the airwaves and the internet. After a few seconds it was drowned out by the voice of WCBN Radio: "It's eleven o'clock. The city is dark, but the fire burns. It burns in the offices. It burns on Wall Street. It burns in the City. It burns on the Bund. It burns in Dubai. It burns in the factories and power plants. And it burns within us. Because we are the business and we all need redemption. This is the hour of delusion and today's truth. This is The Boardroom. Here is your prophet, the buddy and the bodyguard of every CEO, the Don Juan of every business babe. Here is the world's one and only bizz jockey. Here is your BJ: Carl Pappas!"

Seated in the studio were three middle-aged men. One of them was, of course, Carl Pappas, the bizz jockey. The other two were guests, glowing with excitement about their imminent performance on the world's most important business news radio program. Yet their glow was partly because Hitomi Sakamoto, the radio producer, had polished their egos with relentless pep talk until they shone like halos, and because they wore handmade suits of pure silk. Even their hair and chins were shining. One was arranging his cufflinks with an unmoved face, the other dabbed the sweat off his forehead and polished his eyebrows, which were already drenched. He was possibly suffering from stage fright by proxy for his host. But there was no need for that. A switch had been turned on in Carl Pappas; as soon as the WCBN Radio voice fell silent he exploded with a volume, a tempo and a fire that caused even the coolest of the two guests to open his eyes wide.

"Men and women of the business, welcome to The Boardroom, where just like any other day we ask ourselves: where do we stand? If you know the answer, you may call now. But don't take this lightly; many went before you. Many were mistaken. And are grounded now, in court, in jail or in hell. A few moments from now I will introduce tonight's guests, who are already sweating on the other side of the microphone. But first... And yes, we have our first caller. This is Carl Pappas in The Boardroom, can I help you?"

"Hi, this is John."

"John, where are you?"

"I'm in Shanghai right now, but I'm from Columbus, Ohio."

"Sounds like a major step forward, John. What do you do?"

"CEO of a pharmaceutical multinational."

"You sound like you're on pills yourself, John."

"I..."

"Pills are for losers, John."

"Let's hope you have some pharmacy shares, Carl. You always ask where we stand, well: we're taking the price of our shares through the roof today."

"What's this, you are calling me with good news? I've just been announced as the prophet, the bodyguard, every CEO's buddy. Come and bother me with a problem, OK? Give me something to chew on."

"Yes. OK. Listen. One of our best selling pills probably has... a side effect."

"Dammit, John!"

Hitomi Sakamoto grew pale behind the window. She curled her upper lip at the thought of the penalty for cursing she would receive being the producer of Pappas' show.

"What should I do? If word gets out we're going to the dogs."

"And rightfully so. Why do you keep such stuff to yourselves?"

"We didn't know. It's a long-term effect."

"So what is this side effect exactly?"

"I daren't say."

Pappas rose from his chair as if stung by a bee. He yanked at his hair, pointed down to the presentation table with his outstretched arm. "This is precisely what's wrong with this world. This is why corporate America and corporate Europe have such a hopeless reputation. Never take any responsibility. Never take a good look at ourselves first."

"Now wait a minute."

"Your kind ruins it for everybody else, John. And it's so easy. Do every CEO in the world a favor. And all the people that buy your pills. Get it on CNN, plead guilty."

"That isn't an option."

"Yes it is. Swallow ten of your dumb pills publicly. Accepting the money while washing your hands in innocence. Bye bye John. Is John really your name?"

"No of course not. Don't you have a better advice, Pappas?

No brilliant PR escape stunt?"

"You must think I'm joking. Listen, you're not telling me what the side effects are, so how am I to give you advice? The worse the side effect is the sooner you must come out with this story. Sooner or later it will become public knowledge and then you'll be torn to pieces. If you call CNN now and clear your conscience and start worrying about the people who've bought your garbage, you may still stand a chance. That's my advice."

"My lawyers say..."

"Your lawyers know about this? You're a basket case, John. But listen, could I take one of your pills too? Suddenly I don't feel so well."

"No. It's only for... err... young women."

"Dirty geezer! Selling bad pills to teenagers. How long have you known about this, John?"

"A week."

"Get it out. Don't wait. It's your responsibility. Your whole life evolves around this moment, John: protect the consumer. Be a hero. If it kills your career it kills your career. Be a man."

He made a gesture that said as much as: decapitate. Don terminated the connection with the caller. Pappas sat down again, but kept his face close to the Shure SM7, the black, long, vertically positioned microphone that Don Wozniak called the beast. The Shure SM7 excelled in oppressing the surrounding noise and was perfect for a radio guy like Pappas who liked to speak close to the microphone, who spoke a lot, and loudly at that.

"People, stay on the lookout for John, wait for his confession on CNN and give him a hard applause and your support. He'll be needing it badly. But first some messages and then we'll be back with our guests. They're sitting opposite me and have been ready for quite a while, but of course we have to wait for our Mystery Guest, who's due any minute. This is Carl Pappas. This is WCBN Radio. This is The Boardroom."

Hitomi Sakamoto sighed with relief (be it without a sound; she did everything in her power to avoid attracting the sound engineer's attention). We're up and running, she thought. Even after all these years as a producer a certain stage fright consumed her at the start of The Boardroom, the show with which bizz jockey Carl Pappas attracted listeners from the worldwide business community; even if she knew Pappas always did the right things, never fell silent, never made judgment errors, never allowed himself to be silenced by anyone. There was simply no reason to feel tension, and yet she felt it. That's who Hitomi Sakamoto was.

"A DJ has a psychiatrist in his show," said Don Wozninak, the sound engineer, without looking at her.

"Oh no," moaned Hitomi.

"The DJ asks: glad you're here. What do you think of my show? Says the psychiatrist: unfortunately that falls under medical confidentiality."

"I don't get it."

"It's a teaser, Sakamoto."

"You always say that when you tell a stupid joke, Donald Lech Wozniak," bitched Hitomi. She had the stubborn habit of addressing her male colleagues by their full birthnames, which perfectly suited her authoritarian approach of her job.

Being the producer of Carl Pappas' radio show The Boardroom she needed a lot of authority, if only to put overaged brats like Don Wozniak to work for her. It annoyed her that she and Wozniak were regularly mentioned in one breath, as if they were the ideal couple. Like brother and sister. Like top athletes in a team that runs like clockwork. Like a couple that can read each other's minds. Nothing was further from the truth; Don and Hitomi did not look identical, they did not speak the same language, did not empathize with each other and bumped into each other regularly because neither of them wanted to step aside for the other. Don the slob, the chaotic, the asshole. Don who left coffee-dipped doughnuts all over the place making everything sticky, smoked on the roof of the WCBN Radio building and took the smell back inside, if not the cigarette itself. Don who delivered irrelevant information without interruption from his unshaven, fluffy face, pale from life indoors, his thin, sticky but still pitch-black hairs pointing in multiple directions. His way too large glasses (token of respect to his favorite television series The Thunderbirds) continuously sliding towards the tip of his nose, just like his trousers continuously slid down over the slit of his buttocks, much to the horror of Hitomi, who was also confronted by his oversized T-shirts that allowed Don's belly to crawl to the light. There will be no further mention of his remarkably thick lips, always smeared with whipping cream or some other substance such as pieces of cigarette paper, nor will we get into the state of his gym shoes.

The contrast with Hitomi, immaculately dressed and presented, could hardly be greater. She basically treated all her colleagues with a certain disdain, which had an additional advantage: men would think twice before coming close to her. Don Wozniak, like any man, kept his hands to himself these days because he had once gripped into the prickles of an exotic belt girded around Hitomi's paper-thin waist, and had behaved like an idiot, waving his bloody hand, and exposed himself before the entire studio staff as the only man who had dared to touch the deadly beast belt of Hitomi. He still looked, but only from the corner of his eyes, always suspicious, always checking if the producer was wearing any dangerous clothes. Hitomi always looked back at him and gave him a deadly grin that meant as much as: look, but don't touch.

Hitomi Sakamoto spent her leisure time in the gym, the swimming pool and the city park and dressed in a such way that no one could remain oblivious to the fact that her muscles were the result of hard labor and not of sheer youth; after all she was just past forty. In the right light this was all pretty obvious. One might say she did it on purpose. Some actually said this, by the way.

"Now be quiet again," said Hitomi. "I have to concentrate."

The alert tigress inside her had awoken, guarding of the well-being of the beast Carl Pappas. The man who could say anything he liked on the radio; and step on some very long toes along the way. Hitomi Sakamoto waited for these moments, because they were good for business at WCBN Radio. And hence they were good for her career.

Two

"It's Monday night. It's half past eleven. Tonight, as usual for every fortnight here in The Boardroom, is Mystery Hour. Two CEOs. One Mystery Guest. Fifteen minutes. You are all witnesses. Listen to how they react. Listen for the one who keeps a clear head and for the one who abandons ship. Who saves face? Who walks the talk? You decide. Your referee: Carl Pappas."

The first half hour was wrapped up. Several listeners had called and had interesting, shocking, informative and insulting conversations with Carl. The mood was good. His two guests, the two middle-aged, greying gentlemen in executive suits, were in peak condition, although they had not really contributed to the show yet.

The bizz jockey erupted in the prolonging of his program. "Two CEOs are seated next to each other on the plane. They're flying business class, what else would you expect? Great leg room they got here, says one of them. Not nearly enough for the legs of my new girlfriend, says the other. And that's how it is, people. There can only be one boss. One's a loser, one's a winner!"

A drumroll sounded in the studio. The men in suits knew this was the sign for them.

"A warm and professional welcome for my guests. You already heard them laugh in the background a couple of times, but let me introduce them to you now: Olof Stockholm and Bernard Topanga," rattled Carl. "Two CEOs. Two men. Two multinationals. Gentlemen, we have a short span of attention here at WCBN. Q&A in telegram style. Olof Stockholm: CEO of what and why?"

Olof Stockholm, the iciest of the two men, the one without sweat on his forehead, answered as if performing on radio was his true profession: "I run a conglomerate of companies, that all together deal in everything from raw materials to end product. The end product being silicones and I do it because silicones make many women and men happy and because raw materials will soon be unaffordable. So there's a real challenge."

"Bernard Topanga: CEO of what and why?"

"CEO of a company that produces polypropylene for end users, that is from raw material to usable basis, because I am a people's manager and enjoy getting engineers, factory workers and chemists to work together."

"We've got two doctor Frankensteins in the studio, people. They're dreaming that you pull out your wallet to have your wife stuffed with silicones in order to make her fashionable just a few more years, on the couch with her tablet in a designer polypropylene sleeve."

"I think there are some of our raw materials in the chair you're sitting in, mister Pappas," Bernard Topanga noted.

"No need to get personal right away, Bernard. The listeners

didn't tune in to this show to get to know me. They want to get to know you! So I'm going to interrupt you, because this is the moment our third guest arrives. My charming producer Hitomi is going to install our Mystery Guest, we'll be right back."

While Pappas leaned back and winked to the two men in suits at the other side of the table, and a musically accompanied female voice started to elaborate on a deodorant, the door swung open and Hitomi entered, followed closely by a woman of an entirely different nature. The men looked her up and down while she seated herself. Hitomi poured a glass of water and put it on the table in front of the newcomer and immediately disappeared through the door again. Behind the glass Don raised ten fingers. His voice sounded in the studio: "The commercial ends in five seconds, four, three..."

During the last two seconds Carl grinned at his three table companions and took off. "In the mean time our Mystery Guest has arrived in the studio. Well, I'd say: introduce yourself."

The woman started talking, but Olof and Bernard had a little trouble focusing at first. For a few moments they continued staring at the woman on the opposite side of the table, on the bizz jockey's left, there faces mimicking a boxing champion's coach who sees his protégé go down in the first round and tons of prize money evaporate. The woman fitted the tiny bit category. A tiny bit too much makeup. A tiny bit too much emphasis on the hair, a little bit too blond. A tiny bit too much teeth. Her dress a tiny bit too tight, considering her weight, and her lips a tiny bit too much. But never more than that tiny bit; she had stopped just before becoming common. It must also be stated that her voice left nothing to complain; her pronunciation was as sharp as a knife and she spoke with a comforting, warm sound, never shrill, at the most a tiny bit too deep, as often happens to women from real life who've forgotten to stop smoking and drinking on time. The first two sentences the woman spoke were lost on the two men, but they came around just in time to pick up the thread when Carl Pappas responded to his Mystery Guest's words.

"Great to have you here, Victoria. Listeners, Victoria is the woman of my dreams, well, one of the women of my dreams anyway. Listen to that voice, you could be part of a vocal backing group for all I know. And it's a good thing your legs are hidden beneath the table here in The Boardroom, Victoria."

Victoria laughed at Carl and then switched to a *killer smile* for the two other guests.

"The question we all should ask ourselves is of course: Olof, Bernard, do you know Victoria? Ever seen her? Honest..."

"Never!" said Bernard loud.

"Now there's a clear answer. I hadn't even finished yet. You, Olof?"

"I've never seen this lady before, but I must admit that doesn't mean much, because a lot of women look like that."

"Do you talk to your employees like that too, Olof? What's wrong with the way Victoria looks? You don't think she's... she's..."

"Whorish?" yelled Victoria with obvious joy.

"You didn't hear me use that word."

"No, because you used other words to say it."

"I mean the lady had her hair bleached and uses makeup and clothes in a fashionable way, and there are many..."

Carl interrupted him rudely. "Victoria, we have established that the gentlemen do not know you, which makes you a true Mystery Guest. But if you think, listener, that this wraps it up, you're wrong. Victoria is about to reveal the reason for her visit, because this is not a cozy talkshow, this is were scandals are raked up out of the mud, cesspools are emptied, tough nuts are cracked, problems solved and truths slammed on the wall."

Don flew in a short jingle with a sexy vocal group singing "Mysteryyy, mysteryyy, mystery gueeeest."

"I say Victoria take it away!"

"I work in a network of call girls and gigolos that was started by and for CEOs."

"If it wasn't for me talking right now, people, you'd be hearing an awkward silence in the studio this very moment," roared Carl Pappas.

"In the worldwide community of CEOs, but also CFOs, CMOs..."

"Yes yes, we're getting your point Victoria."

"In the worldwide business community a need arose for an organization that operated with a little more privacy and confidentiality. There was a time when top brass could get a brief relationship anywhere, when no one was interested, but ever since DSK things have become delicate."

"Speak clearly for áll listeners, Victoria."

"She means Strauss-Kahn," said Bernard Topanga, his voice sounding irritated. "Which seems to be a sexist point of view."

"Explain yourself Bernard," said the host keenly.

"Strauss-Kahn jumped women, got them drunk, imposed himself and worse. That is something different altogether."

"Something different than... what?" said Pappas. He looked cheerfully at his guest, who swiped sweat drops off his forehead.

"Something different than whatever this lady is talking about."

"Oh well, sex and the CEO, who cares how that's brought up?"

"I have to agree with my table companion here. DSK was an unrivalled scandal, but of a totally different nature."

"Stop whining boys," snarled Carl. "In that same period of time several top brass characters were demolished through their contacts with call girls. I remember that this top golf player..."

"Tiger Woods!" shrieked Victoria. "I believe he only committed adultery. He didn't pay for it."

"The only bill he ever got is the one from his wife," laughed Olof Stockholm.

"I don't see much difference myself, but let's give the mike back to Victoria. You're really saying that a CEO who wanted to swing it discretely was taking too much of a risk."

"Yes. The stakes have become too high when CEOs are involved. If you have a cold, Olof, the stock exchange starts to cough," said Victoria, while looking Olof Stockholm straight in the eye. He nodded unmoved, though with a faint smile. "Only a specialized network understands the risks and can ensure that the client's identity always remains a secret."

"Specialized pimps!" shouted Pappas.

"Sounds reasonable," muttered Olof Stockholm.

"Sounds like the biggest nonsense of the past decade. Who'd want to make use of it?" shouted Bernard Topanga, who was becoming visibly irritated.

"Do pay attention, Bernard," snarled Carl. "You would."

By now Topanga's forehead was so dreadfully soaked that even his eyebrows could no longer hold the sweat. He took off his glasses and wiped his face with a handkerchief. "I object to this witch hunt. It's an embarrassment to the CEO community, as if we haven't been suffering a bad image for years already. I'd like to say this: not every investment advisor is a Bernard Madoff."

"And I'd like to say this: power corrupts," said Victoria, perfectly imitating an ice queen.

"What do you mean corrupts?" said Olof Stockholm joining the fray between Victoria and Bernard.

"Yes how do you feel about all this, Olof," poked the host.

Beyond the glass of the studio the faces of Don and Hitomi grinned, although the latter looked sideways immediately, observing the sound engineer laughing at the same thing as she did wiped the smile right off her face.

"I do believe Victoria."

"Oh, done some business with her network?"

"Nice try, Carl. Look, she does have to deliver some sort of proof in your show, but that's your problem, this is your program. I believe her for her brown eyes. If you're a CEO, everything you do is weighed carefully. You cannot go down with flu as then the shareholders will be on the evening news. You cannot make a mistake or you face a hearing. And above all you cannot afford to have a bit on the side. So you have to mistrust everybody. But what if there's a club that has shielded itself off exclusively, wouldn't there be a market for it?" And to that Stockholm added, after a short break, expressively: "Wouldn't there, Topanga?"

Topanga responded agitated: "Mister Stockholm mistakes me for someone who's an expert in this matter. My advice to everyone in a delicate position would be to avoid doing anything that could compromise you in the public's opinion. Madame Victoria."

"Victoria to you, Bernard."

"If you have a rolodex full of exclusive call girls, what keeps you from blackmailing your clients? Would that not be much more lucrative?"

"No, of course not. That wouldn't do my word of mouth recommendations any good now would it? I want one client to introduce the other. What you're saying really is too stupid for words."

"Now we're getting somewhere."

"Basically you're saying I'm lying, mister Topanga."

"Yes. I'd be careful," laughed Olof Stockholm. "If Victoria here says you're a client of hers, go ahead and try to explain that to the press in the morning."

"Come on, Victoria, out with it. Are these two gentlemen clients of your company too? Of your exclusive service? Of your *ladies*?"

"Or of my gigolos, because they're part of the team too," shrieked Victoria. "One for your wife perhaps, Bernard?"

The freaked out businessman, about to put his glasses back on his nose, stuck the arm of his glasses in his eye, mumbled a curse, and stood up. They all laughed at him. Even the host was at a loss of words while Bernard Topanga desperately tried to escape the wires of his headphones that seemed to chain him to the table.

There was something about the tormented face of Topanga that seemed to soften Victoria. She put up a calming voice.

"Bernard take it easy and sit down because I'm not trying to make a fool out of you. The girls who work for me are really there for men like you and that's not all about money. They all admire the CEOs of the world. Their tough position in the world of money. How they try to combine their hard business life with the vulnerability of their families."

"Those girls of yours sound like real groupies to me!" yelled Carl Pappas into the microphone with the perfect diction that goes with a radio slogan.

"I choose them for that. In this respect I am CEO groupie number one and I know exactly what you like, Bernard."

The last sentence appeared like lingerie from a tumble dryer, but it failed to have the desired effect on Bernard Topanga. He yanked his headphone wire into a rain of sparks and made across the corner of the table, towards Victoria and grabbed her throat. He uttered several incoherent cries, which mingled with the cries of Carl, Olof and Victoria, made an adequate reproduction of the panic in the studio for the audience.

While Don Wozniak and Hitomi Sakamoto rushed in to separate the embroiled guests, Carl Pappas straightened his back and grinned from ear to ear. This was his show. This was another one of those moments when the ratings were pinpointed at a high level for weeks to come and his salary was secured once again.

"You heard it, dear people. We leave you now for some messages from our sponsors. I hope they're in line with tonight's topic. Next we'll be talking to Victoria, to Olof and hopefully to Bernard, who's desperately trying to escape at the moment. Never a good idea to walk away from a live program so sit down Bernard. Remember, running from a fire leaves a bad impression on the stock exchange!"

Three

Never before had Carl Pappas seen a guest this frightened. She'd been sitting at the table in his office, shaking helplessly. The coffee had restored some of her strength and she'd stopped crying, but her makeup was coming off and her hands were shaking too much to do anything about that. Fortunately there was Hitomi Sakamoto.

"Carl Evangelos Pappas! Get lost. Can't you see Ms. Victoria needs to be alone for a moment, without the company of men?"

"It seems to me the company of a man who understands..."

"Lo-host, Pappas."

Hastily he left the spot and headed to Don's doghouse. The sound engineer was looking for his cell phone. He always put it down somewhere upon arrival and covered it with paperwork and CD boxes and candy wrappers during the broadcast. He was unmoved as ever.

"Oh Carl, call my cell phone, will you? Need to find it."

"Course, Don. But do you have a moment. I'm sort of stuck with that Victoria."

"Don't be stuck with her, Pappas. Let Ratata deal with it."

"The woman's scared out of her wits. You allowed complete *psychos* into the show. Perhaps we overdid it."

"It's not your fault she's upset because of some caller who says he likes to show here a good time with his Black & Decker?"

"It was all right until that caller started to explain in detail what would happen if she visited his place, how he would show her his house and leave a piece of her in every room. It took me a while to get what was going on and by that time it was too late. Everybody was sitting there being all pale. Next thing I know there's a commercial for a *health spa* coming through! Man, am I going to get my ass kicked for that."

"You're not yourself, Carl. Since when do you worry about the sponsors? That's the territory of Phil..."

"I do not need to hear that name right now!"

Of all nights the boss of WCBN Radio, Phil Solo, or Philemon Solo to his friends, had to choose tonight to be absent. But he would undoubtedly have been listening and was probably busy trying to get through the crowded telephone lines, to shout abuse at Don Wozniak and threaten to sack him. Pappas and Sakamoto would shout back abuse and Wozniak would usually allow these rants to shower him, a reaction interpreted by Solo as an act of submissiveness. But the cell phone made no sound.

"The battery's empty, Wozniak."

The sound engineer threw papers around. "Without that thing Alexandra will not be able to get through to me."

"I thought things would have gone differently. That Victoria would not be wiped off her feet so easily."

"Don't tell me Victoria is really her name. Ah, here it is.

Damn! How can that battery be empty already? You have to lend me a battery charger, Carl. Say... what are you standing there for? Go take that Victoria home before Phil gets here, he'll only make things worse."

They looked at each other.

And raised a finger and said simultaneously: "Phil is a client of hers!"

Hitomi stuck her head around the door. "Playing time is over, boys. We got things to do here. Solo is on his way. There's also one of these CEOs hanging around, that Stockholm. He's with Victoria right now. I don't like that sticking around. He's up to something and I don't need that."

"He's not a sucker for forty-something Japanese women, Hitomi."

"Nor for thirty-five something unshaven *nerds*, Wozniak. All right Pappas, what will it be?

"Send that Stockholm guy home. Make up an excuse. I'll take Victoria home."

The parking garage roof shone in the night. Carl had put his overcoat around her shoulders, Hitomi held an umbrella over her head and so they brought Victoria to Pappas' car. She got in, Hitomi closed the door.

"Listen Carl Evangelos. Don't you think I should ride along?"

"For crying out loud Sakamoto. You worried she might hit on me or something?"

She rolled her eyes.

"Listen, Í caused all this by inviting her. Things turned out differently, I have to take her home. I mean: she has been threatened. And quite seriously too."

The wind began to stir. Hitomi moved and stood closer to him than she had ever done before. He thought he felt her breasts through his jacket.

"OK, bring her home. Make a left turn six times. If you see a car following you, don't drive to her home but to a police station."

"Huh?"

"A security measure. Something you should do after every broadcast."

He sighed.

And got in.

With squeaking tires his Mercedes, an old timer that existed outside of every environmental law and noise standard, moved towards the exit and dived downward. He turned into the street, alongside the WCBN Radio building. It was there that the noise was reduced slightly and that the car stopped spitting stinking clouds.

"Thank you, Pappas. I'm already feeling better. That studio... It made me claustrophobic, I think that was it. That one of the maniacs would enter the studio, I thought, and there will be nowhere to go. But now, outside... It's getting better. I'm all right now."

"OK."

"I've listened to your show sometimes, but I've never heard something like this. These *psychos*! Do you think... Do you think I should worry about it?"

"No. Barking dogs seldom bite. They call every once and a while. If every threat I've heard through the years, live during the broadcast, had been executed, I would be a mosaic in a museum by now. A thousand pieces glued together."

That offered some relief. Victoria laughed.

"You seemed to me a kind of younger version of Margaret Thatcher. A sexy Iron Lady who takes no notice of anyone, who holds tough businessmen in the palm of her hand. And then you allow two callers to knock you off your feet."

"That Bernard went for my throat, don't forget that. Have I disappointed you?"

"Absolutely not. Tomorrow all the world will be listening, because other stations will pick this up. But I didn't want to put a burden on you. I'd feel bad if it would get to you. Then I wouldn't have started this, you see."

"I thought you were untouchable."

"Under normal circumstances I think: your problem, you should not have appeared on my show. Some people you can't break because they are scrap already. But you..."

Pappas' voice switched off, he pushed a dashboard button. Soft soul flowed into the Mercedes.

"You're OK, Pappas. You have a big mouth, but you are not as bad as your guests."

The BJ grinned while he started the first of the six left turns as prescribed by Hitomi Sakamoto. He looked in the rearview mirror but saw nothing.

Four

The alarm clock abruptly opened the day. Carl Pappas had not
woken up this way in years. While he stared through his wide
open eyes, astonished and paralyzed, and tried to develop a
clear thought about the way he would scold and then fire his
housemaid (there was no doubt about her guilt of the
disastrous result of her touching the alarm clock), he tried to
tune in to whatever the extremely loud voice of the
announcer was proclaiming.

"...and all around there have been dismal responses to the
flood of abuse in bizz jockey Carl Pappas' show at WCBN
Radio. I will now play a fragment. But here's a warning first.
For sensitive listeners the following soundbite can be
shocking; if you are one of..."

"Man, cut that crap," moaned Pappas.

The room stretched around him in relative half-light. The
curtains blocked the daylight except for a narrow slit where
the sun peeked in. The vague ray of daylight was dampened
further by the dark upholstery of the room: a black carpet,
black duvet on the bed and dark red walls. Across the full
width of the wall, at the head of the bed, hung a painting that

expressed a passionate spirit, loaded with exploding sunflowers that gave way to women's breasts. The wall opposite of the foot of the bed had disappeared behind a series of closet doors, again dark red. In the corner opposite of the door was a small sitting area with a low table with a telephone and a large bouquet of flowers, and two fauteuils. This room was firmly reminded of the interior architect's original intentions on a daily basis.

Carl Pappas recognized his own voice on the radio. The previous night returned. It appeared he was answering an incoming phone call during the broadcast.

"This is Carl Pappas. Go ahead, Harold?"

"Shall we play a game, Pappas?" The man coughed in a strange high-pitched way.

He sighed. "Course Harold. What is this, a game show? I'm the godfather of the top brass and you want to play a game? That's why I've got ten million listeners and you have nóthing. It's a good thing I'm all for freedom of speech so take it away."

"Thank you, Pappas. It's a game for Victoria. I make a sound and she can guess what it is."

"Just get on with it Harold."

"No I need to know if she's in. Will you play the game, Victoria?"

"Are you a CEO, Harold?"

The caller had not counted on that. He coughed again, a nervous, hiccup-like way of coughing. The answer came in a stutter. "N-n-no... But th-that is irrelevant. Here we go. Guess the sound!"

Through the phone a rattle sounded, a rapid series of thuds

and then clearly a chainsaw. Loud and unmistakably.

"You hear that Victoria!" shouted the caller through all this. "Soon there will be two of you! Whore!"

"Another fine moment," Carl interrupted the caller, but he could not prevent the man from shouting "I know where you live!" quickly before he was cut off by Don Wozniak. "Thanks, Harold. Same to you."

Wrestling the duvet with his entangled legs Carl crawled towards the alarm clock to launch it from the night table with a blow of his fist. The cracking noise that came from out of his sight did not deliver the end of the radio transmission he had anticipated. The breakfast show announcer's voice coolly picked up where he had left off.

"The question is now: how did it come to this? Phil Solo, chairman of WCBN Radio said this morning that this is one of the risks of live shows, but in the political arena the responses are agitated. Is this really necessary, asks the US Secretary of Commerce. Do the men and women who pull the chariot of the nation through the mud of the international economy really have to be mocked at in this fashion? And the IMF chairman asks if now the time is ripe for a new kind of immunity for people who put so much of their lives at jeopardy to raise our gross national product? Also the threatened woman here, Victoria, deserves protection. Can she count on a police escort to shield her from possible psychopaths or is Carl Pappas, the self-proclaimed bizz jockey, looking the other way? It's an outrage..."

A dry click; the radio fell silent. Carl made a big effort to look up and saw his girlfriend's long legs. There were days when Carl Pappas failed to remember her name instantly.

Days when he could not summon up her face instantly. Days when a man has to rely on the legs. This was one of those days.

"Thank you, darling. You saved my life once again."

"Good morning. The *ratings* are going through the roof, Carl. Rise and shine."

"Says who?"

"Says Phil. He just called but I turned him down."

"I wonder if they pour coffee after the apocalypse," asked Carl.

"Only for those who are of use. So you'll be all right. Stay where you are and you'll get coffee and something else."

She disappeared. He grinned. For a moment he cherished the thought of her returning with coffee and something else, but the previous night imposed itself on him. He remembered how he had delivered Victoria at her apartment at the other side of Chinatown, a neighborhood consisting mainly of condominiums for the upper middle class. The group that was not rich enough to live off their investments, but prosperous enough to enjoy the riches of life. The entrance of the complex was lit in the night like a 52nd Avenue restaurant on Christmas Eve; the night porter sat behind his teak counter and nodded affably, but expressionless, without signs of curiosity. Carl remembered how pleasant this felt, how mild mannered when compared to the porters of the complex where he himself resided, rude impertinent hulks without necks, dressed in uniforms and either entirely disinterested — even if you could use a little help dragging your suitcase — or overtly curious. Whenever he walked a female guest to the elevator you knew for sure that the porter, irrespective which one of them, would stare after you, or enter the elevator in a hurry. In that sense walking Victoria was a relief. The light appeared to be coming from candles, there was the soft music of the likes of Vivaldi and the porter minded his own business. He may have been reading an evening paper. They said goodbye at the elevator, in spite of Carl's insistence.

"There is no need for that whatsoever," Victoria had said. "This building is guarded."

"That man is reading the newspaper," he had said. (Worriedly, because he refused to believe that a psychopath on his way to kill Victoria would actually be stopped by the civilized man behind the counter.) He did not want to make the impression that he liked to go up with Victoria. Carl Pappas had no aversion to women, however he had made it a habit to never become personally involved with guests who had recently appeared in the show. His neutrality was always at stake. Keep a minimum of six months between the broadcast and a personal contact, his lawyer always said.

"Carl, the porter is heavily armed," his guest had whispered.

She had come quite close to him. "Recently an angry man showed up here, he had been fired by one of my neighbors who is head of personnel at some IT company. Rumor has it the porter took control of him with a jujitsu grip and then, just to be certain, put a gun against his head, while he called for police assistance with his left hand."

Carl had laughed about that and left Victoria to go up in the elevator alone. As he had left the building the porter nodded affably again, this time smiling faintly. Was the man wearing his black belt under his suit? Carl had wondered.

He yanked open the curtains, squeezing his eyes while a stab of pain from the light ripped open his irises. Suddenly he was overwhelmed by a powerful longing for the half-light of the studio, for Don Wozniak's smoky cave, for Hitomi Sakamoto's retorts, for Phil Solo's insults.

Tuesday mornings were traditionally reserved for his business brunch with Philemon Solo, managing director of WCBN Radio. For Pappas the rants of Solo were a kind of overpaid whining; on the other hand the man made sure Carl could do his work relatively shielded off from shareholders.

"You and your conscience. If Í had a conscience wé would not have ten million listeners, Philemon," he kicked of in his usual Tuesday way, exactly at the moment when the waitress was within hearing distance. Because at those words she always looked at him with a thick smile, and he liked that. The waitress, Katie, or in full Katharina Yekaterina, at least ever since she was born from two Russian émigré parents, had a wrestler's body, large and muscular, which she compensated for with an exceptional pretty face and beautifully put up hair. Because she was no longer the youngest beauty, approaching fifty — like Carl himself —, she was to him a kind of Russian grand duchess who had temporarily left her country like Peter the Great to serve coffee, soup and sandwiches in this franchise. Naturally the hair was bleached, but other than that she was as real as they come.

"Here in the Gulag no one cares that you have ten million listeners and are therefore filthily rich," snarled.Katie with an accent that, though difficult to pinpoint, probably originated from somewhere between the Volga and the Ganges.

"My beautiful *Lady of the Night*," yelled Carl. "Katharina Yekaterina, how beautiful you look again. You're one hell of a woman. Look at her, Philemon, isn't she beautiful. We can lunch here quietly and not worry about our expensive jackets; here we're just like everybody else thanks to the matrone di matrone, thanks to..."

"Thank you, Pappas. How is coffee for starters? Or have you two decided to better your lives?"

After taking the order she curled her lips gesturing a kiss in Carl's direction, and walked of, into her Gulag, a cozy rectangular cabin with lots of raw wood on the floor and ceilings, heavy doors and unpolished tables. All the windows, including those leading to the kitchen, had iron bars. One of the walls was covered top to bottom with a photo of a Siberian snow landscape, white as a sheet with the dark edge of a forest on the horizon.

"The good news is that the ratings went through the roof last night."

"I guess the bad news is that the WCBN roof will be repaired at my expense?"

"Not very funny, Carl. You are not top-notch this morning. Oh well, the day is still young. Let's hope your time will come today. The bad news is that we are facing some extremely bad publicity. The number of complaints coming in is breaking all records. Worse: there's pressure from the powers that be."

Carl smiled. This coincided with the approach of Katie, who was bringing the coffee. She returned the smile. Confused, he shook his face back in its normal, uninterested mode. "Pressure, Phil. How very interesting. The audience share is rising, so they're getting more money upstairs, and what do they do? They put pressure on you."

"More money? I'm not so sure. You think sponsors need a riot or shit? A government secretary has complained on television. The IMF has made noise. Next thing I know some censorship committee is all over me. You know what that is, Carl? And what's that you're throwing into your coffee, Carl? Don't you know that's bad for you? What is that: a creamer? Sugar?"

The bizz jockey tiredly waved, signing him to continue.

"You know what the committee dude was telling me this morning? He started by saying that they had listened to the tape of the broadcast on the orders of the state secretary and had noted ten cases of clandestine advertising and blasphemy, or something like that, at fifty thousand a piece. That is five-hundred grand in fines, if they feel like it."

"They won't."

"No. Not if I cooperate, they won't. But it's still a hassle. The guys upstairs don't like that, because if word gets out we're under the lamp the sponsors start looking for the exit. They pay your..."

"Salary, yes."

He had finished stirring his coffee.

"It's always the same old song, Phil. The more hurly-burly the show, the more listeners and the more money; the more they complain and kiss ass because there's cursing or whatever. After that they simply take their money and there's silence all over again."

"This is more serious than that, Carl. Nasty things were said last night. Things people don't like. To tell you the truth

I'm not too proud myself that a guest in your show is threatened with chainsaws and that CEO groupies are the main topic. Look, you make a critical show, so you don't have to start being cozy. But I agree this is... indelicate."

"Indelicate. What a word," said Carl. And then to Katie, who was bringing sandwiches: "He understands it, doll. He understands that the angrier the listeners are, the more of them we'll see and the longer the commercial breaks will be."

"Hey, even I understand that," laughed Katie, and she curled her upper lip to Phil Solo, who looked crestfallen.

"You're getting pressure from above," said Carl. "Good. Consider the alternative: you're getting nó pressure from above. Now thére's something to worry about."

Five

The Friday night was not Carl's favorite broadcast night. The weekend leaned heavily against this hour. The listeners longed to get a break from the economic ratrace. Through the years the contents of The Boardroom in the week's final episode had been slightly adjusted to better suit the inevitable listener's fatigue. The accent was more on the other side of business life: less delicate subjects, more focus on entertainment. Movie stars and fashion designers worked better than any other topic on Friday; which didn't mean that the bizz jockey had to abandon his acerbity.

No way.

"This is The Boardroom. Here is your prophet, the buddy and the bodyguard of every CEO, the Don Juan of every business babe. Here is the world's one and only bizz jockey. Here is your BJ: Carl Pappas!" (And immediately followed by Carl's voice:) "My dear, dear business friends, welcome to Friday night. We have to take the vote here in the studio. My tough producer and representative, the only one who keeps the outside world at bay, the best Chinese Wall a celebrity can wish for, although she's actually Japanese: Hitomi. And my own Luke Skywalker of the radio waves, our unmatched sound engineer Don. The three of us have watched the stocks and the conclusion this week is: you all made the grade. Now don't start thinking too high about yourselves right now; now one is really sailing home on the prices of shares, but the trend was upward. Which means..."

A wide smile appeared on the face of Don Wozniak, who had opened a can of beer to raise it in his left hand, pointing to the bizz jockey, while pushing a control with his other hand, causing a drumroll and some trumpet sounds in the studio.

"Yes, that means that we're going to play a record. The old fashioned way, like they used to in school: when you were good, miss teacher would put on a movie or mister teacher would read from T.E. Lawrence, like they used to in my childhood, or, and I have mercy on you, from Harry Potter if you were born in another time. Your bad luck. Don, let's hear it."

Don Wozniak's smile broadened, while he looked around him for the producer. But she was standing in one of the other rooms that looked out at the recording studio, in the half-light. She stood there talking to Phil Solo, but to Don's pleasure he saw her cast a look in his direction, irritated when the first sounds of Rod Stewart's "Passion" echoed from the speakers.

As soon as Don reduced the volume, at the end of the song, and slowly let it fade, Carl took off again.

"Remember, people, if you don't do it with passion, it's not going to work. Bill Gates could sit and write programs for hundreds of hours in a row, don't forget that. The only successful character in history who built his empire on hate, was... Well, you can fill it in."

The music had dissolved and Carl held his breath for a moment for maximum effect.

"Tonight the chairlady of the world's greatest television producer speaks of her passion. Ariana and I — she and I call each other by our first names, yes — will talk about her passion and it is nót watching television. Well, this will surprise no one in The Boardroom, because anyone who wants to achieve anything is not sitting in front of the tube, that place is reserved for the consumers who have to pay for all this. But now we kick off with the question we ask ourselves every day: where do we stand? Don't make a mistake: many went before you, many were mistaken and are grounded now or in court or walking around in iron chains. Ah, it's the first caller. This is Carl Pappas in The Boardroom. Go ahead?"

"Pappas, nice to meet you, this is Geoffrey, I'm an actor."

"Ah, a different sound. What do you play, Geoffrey?"

"Shakespeare."

"Well well, the level of this show is always on the rise on Friday nights. My compliments, Geoffrey. What's your favorite part?"

"King Lear. But I suggest you ask this question to tonight's guest."

"You mean Ariana Abrahamson? We could, yes. Why's that interesting, Geoffrey, and what's that got to do with where we're standing in the world?"

"I'll explain, Pappas."

"I'd hurry if I were you, because your specific gravity is

being reduced at an awful speed."

"I think her favorite part is Lady MacBeth, Pappas. Ariana Abrahamson's television conglomerate is responsible for the avalanche of empty-headed real life shows that have reduced the audience to a brainless mass that does nothing but look at the private lives of quarrelers."

"Big deal, Geoffrey."

"The consequence of which is, moreover, that the masses also need to know nothing but intimate details of the lives of politicians. Even this is provided for by the program makers of her company: at least half of all news shows focus on private scandals of politicians. Who are then rolled in the mud so severely that their reputations are damaged for the rest of their careers. The result being that no successful businessman or woman wants to enter politics now. And these people are badly needed in..."

"Thaaank you King Lear," roared Carl, while he gestured with his hand, flat at his throat, for Don to end the telephone conversation. Which happened immediately.

"For some reason I suspect this'll be a tiresome evening," sighed the bizz jockey in the microphone.

He saw the can in his sound engineer's hand. Could that be... a beer?

Worthless: beer. No, a kingdom for a whiskey. He tried not to look at the clock but to no great avail. The weekend was knocking at the door and had no intention of being kept out much longer.

———

The city had a hangover. It was a good thing it was Saturday morning, so no one was really bothered. Buildings higher than five stories were entangled in a motionless fog. The streets were busy like a weekday, but instead of rushing to their jobs people headed for the do-it-yourself stores, the furniture store boulevards, the warehouses and the gyms for their Saturday activities. Their faces did not betray which day it was.

Carl had dropped off his girlfriend downtown and had retreated hastily to the Gulag. There he sat, as he always did, with a cup of coffee and the weekend newspapers nosing around in the news. Although he had his own editorial staff he deemed it important to be better informed than them. It came down to him coughing up the best ideas himself, usually immediately after his Saturday sessions in the Gulag.

He'd only got as far as his second cup of coffee when three men came and stood at his table.

"Carl Pappas of The Boardroom of WCBN Radio?"

"Not Saturdays, no. We're on the air Mondays thru Fridays. Do call WCBN and ask for Mr. Philemon Solo or my producer, Ms. Hitomi Saka..."

"Are you familiar with the whereabouts of Ms. Rosa Colombina, better known as Victoria and in that second capacity also a guest in your show?"

"And you are?"

"Police. Lieutenant Carlsberg. My colleagues Homburg and Koster."

"Man. Do you really need three of you?"

"Have you heard, Mr. Pappas?"

"O excuse me, I thought you were asking me a rhetorical

question. No, I haven't   got a clue where Victoria is. Something the matter?"

"Yes, her family has reported her missing. She hasn't been home in a couple of weeks, her cell phone's not been used and she has not been in contact with her office. Phil Solo said you'd be here this morning. You're the only person in this city who doesn't answer his cell phone."

Carl shoved the newspapers to the side. He mumbled a curse. Coffee and talk are terrible company, he thought, if you're trying to concentrate.

"Sure I answer my cell phone, but only if my sound engineer is calling, or my producer."

"We've yet to question them."

"Leave these people alone. Victoria disappears and you think we at WCBN have got something to do with that?"

The man who'd introduced himself as Carlsberg sat down. The other two walked off. One took a seat at the coffee bar, the other one positioned himself at the entrance.

Carlsberg took off his fedora and stroke his moustache with his hand. This growth on his upper lip proved that he was either a trendsetter or utterly outdated. Considering his light brown raincoat, his hat and his Rolex the latter description would be the most likely; but Carl liked that. The world was full of fashionistas, who imitated movie and television stars continuously and ran to the hairdressers and the boutiques as if by command, or browsed websites. He was aware of the latest fashions himself, he tried to keep up. A man who doesn't keep abreast of the times is hard to find.

"You're the last person seen in the company of Ms. Rosa Colombina."

"Then it seems to me you've solved the case."

Carlsberg stroked his mustache. He gestured to the waitress with his right hand; Katie was off duty on Saturday morning, so the few customers present were served by a girl Carl scarcely knew because he never exchanged a single word with her outside of the order. Carlsberg signaled that two new cups of coffee were needed by drawing a circle over the table with his index finger.

"On the radio you're sure funny, Mr. Pappas," said Carlsberg. "But in real life I like it a lot less, that humor of yours. So do me a favor."

They looked at each other.

Carl shrugged. "I haven't seen her since that night. I brought her home then because she'd been threatened during the show."

"Spoken to her since?"

"Yeah. I called her that week a couple of times to check in on her. She acted rather tough, as if it hadn't touched her, but I've never believed that. She sounded very nervous but resolutely refused protection or anything."

"Received any threats after the broadcast?"

"Threats arrive in truckloads at WCBN," sighed Carl. Usually that made him proud, but this time he felt uncomfortable about it.

"I mean threats addressed to Rosa Colombina."

"Every letter or e-mail with a threat is put aside and destroyed after a while. These are huge piles, I'm not exaggerating. It's a business in its own right. Do you have any idea how much I pay the paper shredding company?"

"A burden you can carry, no doubt. How long do you keep

the mail?"

Carl stared sullenly as the man stroke his mustache and he tried to remember who Carlsberg resembled. Which television actor had such a moustache?

"A month. To the day. But before you ask anything else: I do not read a single letter or e-mail, especially not if there's anything weird in there. I get enough abuse during the broadcasts."

The coffee arrived. They drank silently.

After a while the lieutenant spoke again, but briefly this time.

"In that case I've bad news, Mr. Pappas."

Bad news arrives in all kinds and sizes. There's the kind that announces itself and the kind that comes falling out of thin air. We all have our preferences (in the long run no one escapes bad news) and Carl Pappas preferred the unexpected kind. Well, he had never expected that he and Hitomi Sakamoto would be plowing through mountains of envelopes and a hard disk in the basement of the WCBN building, on an ordinary Saturday afternoon, when they were supposed to be recovering from a week's work. The fact that lieutenant Carlsberg was giving them a hand was scarcely any comfort.

Every now and then one of them broke the silence to read some painful prose from a letter or e-mail received, but in the course of the afternoon this occurred less and less. Hate mail quickly becomes a bore.

By the end of the afternoon Carlsberg took all the mail that was connected to the Victoria broadcast back to the police station to put his people to work on it. Many hate mail writers had stoically written their names and addresses under their message and the police station would look into that. But it did not look like a promising task.

"Why would anybody write his name and address under such a letter and then do something to Victoria? That's hardly logical. He'd be easy to trace, wouldn't he?"

"In my line of work logic is not very important. Psychopaths do the weirdest things. It's just that we have few other places to start," said Carlsberg, while they left the building through the lobby. "Rosa Colombina's apartment shows no traces other than her own. No burglary. The porter has seen nothing of significance."

"Did he see her leave?" asked Hitomi.

"No," said Carlsberg. "But that doesn't mean a lot. Porters take a leak sometimes too, you know."

"You don't know if she left home alone or in the company of someone?"

"No. So we'll investigate two things: all hate mail that was sent to your network and all her business contacts. She had quite a few of them, but what's worse: she was meticulously secretive about it. All we found were heavily encrypted computer files that you are unlikely to decipher in a hundred years. So we have to go with what her employees have memorized. I've got another question though. Would it be possible to get the phone number of everyone who called you during the show?"

"No," said Hitomi. "The Boardroom guarantees the anonymity of all callers. Of course that attracts more lunatics, but it does bring in real top brass who'd otherwise not make the call."

"And whistle-blowers. Don't forget the whistle-blowers," said Carl.

"Not even from the phone company?"

"No, said Hitomi. "Well, you can ask, but you're wasting your time. A deal was struck."

"OK, thanks for your time. Pappas. Sakamoto."

Carl and Hitomi looked at the lieutenant, who stepped into a car that was standing ready on the boulevard in front of the building.

"Carl Evangelos Pappas, are you feeling guilty?" asked Hitomi.

He looked at her, squeezed his eyes. Their collaboration existed of responding wittily to what the other was saying, but he could tell just by looking at her face that there was no trace of sarcasm in her remark.

"No," he said. "But it does piss me off. I'm not responsible for people's actions, I make sure it gets on the radio. But... if you hear in what filthy way some people on the phone speak of others, then... I don't know. I'm so used to it that I no longer think about taking these people seriously. I talk through like it's nothing. And nothing ever happened. But now I'm not so sure anymore. What if someone..."

His voice broke off. They turned around and entered the WCBN building again, passed the counter and approached the elevators.

"I think nothing's the matter. She's just away for a while," said Hitomi in an airy way.

"What makes you think that?"

"The freak who was calling in live and threatened her was simply craving attention. Those types enjoy the fact that everything they say, no matter how disgusting, is heard by ten million listeners all over the world. I don't think someone like that would do something to her and then remain silent about it."

Carl sighed.

"The first thing someone like that would do would be to call again the next day and proudly proclaim, during the live transmission, that he'd done something to her!" said Hitomi triumphantly. Presumably she thought she had a knack for police work.

They took the elevator.

"I'm getting my coat," said Hitomi.

She wanted to push the button of their floor, but Carl stopped her.

"Wait a minute. You may have a point there. We must listen to the broadcast again. We may find a clue."

Hitomi pushed his hand away and resumed pushing the button.

"You do it, Carl." She even forgot his other names.

"Stop bleating, Sakamoto. You ask me if I feel guilty. How about you? If Victoria has really disappeared, doesn't that bother you?"

"I didn't say that. I just think that listening to a Carl Pappas show twice is a bit too much."

Six

"No doubt about it," said Carl. "Just listen."

It was Sunday morning. Don Wozniak, chain smoking over his panels, had been waiting for the signal Carl was now giving him. Inside the studio the bizz jockey and lieutenant Carlsberg were sitting at the table. Wozniak started the file with a fragment of the Victoria broadcast.

"Olof, what's your estimate of the net worth of such a network of exclusive CEO call girls? What kind of turnover would Victoria make on that? And what level of profit? Go on, make an educated guess, because she's obviously not going to give it to us."

Carl talked right through it. "This is where she looked really angry," he said loudly. "Mán did she look angry here."

"If I had to guess from what Victoria has told us so far," said Olof Stockholm through the sound system, "then I reach the following conclusion. And I'd like to include her claim that she operates from five global cities, by which she clearly means New York, Rio, Beijing, Dubai and Berlin. There can't be more than a few dozen of CEOs for clients. Because at the level where a top executive is vulnerable, in the sense that a possible fall from grace is immediately punishable through the stock exchange, you'll find a hundred or two hundred men and women at the most. They won't all become clients, so I'd say you might get thirty or fifty of them. Let's be optimistic here..."

"Or pessimistic!" yelled Bernard Topanga.

"...and presume there'll be fifty. If you're a top girl, you're talking tens of thousands a night and this can be done dozens of times a year. Now let's see..."

"You're talking like a pro here, Olof."

"I have a great wife. She supports me in my work and she's a CEO herself, so she's familiar with the problems of my job. I don't need some skinny fashion model with nothing to say."

"Tough talk, Olof. But you don't need to convince me of anything. What's your estimate?"

"I'd say an easy thirty million a year. Clean profit. I don't know the fee these women are getting, I may be undervaluing them."

"How about you, Victoria."

"I didn't come here to talk about money. You must admit, Carl, that there's never talk about the personal incomes of the guests on this show."

"No, that would scare everybody away for good. But this is a different ballgame, Victoria. We're talking about the enormous amounts that our corporate stratosphere is spending on sex. Oh well, it sounds like it doesn't make much difference with all these billions. What's thirty million on all these top salaries and bonuses?"

"Pay attention now!" shouted Carl right through the recording.

Next spoke Bernard Topanga.

"You people talk like you believe every word this lady is reeling off. But what if every word of it is a lie? I know at least fifteen to twenty percent of the top executives you're talking about here and I absolutely refuse to believe that this ensemble would get involved in something like this. To me this is throwing mud at a professional group that is already suffering from a bad reputation that, mind you, was built by generations before us. The lady would be wise to pay a little more attention to what she's saying before accidents start to happen."

"Accidents, Bernard? Are you threatening Victoria?"

"No. No, but..."

"But what?"

"Madame can not simply throw mud at a professional group. It is called slander and these are not the kind of people who will condone that."

"Should she call her lawyer? Is that what you're saying?"

"Or worse."

"Ah!" yelled Carl. He swept his hand in front of his throat, signaling Don Wozniak to stop the recording. "Caught!"

"Caught?" said Carlsberg hesitatingly. He stroke his moustache with his hand. "Aren't you overdoing it a bit?"

"He threatens her! He says 'or worse'. Isn't that very obvious? He's basically saying that something is going to happen to her that's worse than a lawsuit. The man betrayed himself."

Wozniak entered the room. "Exactly my idea."

"And what do you expect us to do? Go to this Topanga and say, hey mister where'd you hide Victoria?"

"No of course not," said Carl, irritated. "Do we have to spell everything for you? You have to shadow him. Sure he's not going to do it himself, but he's clearly saying on the air that something will happen to Victoria. He's suspicious anyway because he's pissed at this woman all the time. He even grabs her by the throat."

"I'd do that too in your show. You're pissing that man off so that's what you get. That doesn't make him a suspect."

"What kind of proof do you want? The least you must do is investigate him."

"The man's got a top job in the public spotlight. Everybody's paying attention to him. Hardly likely that somebody like him is going to do something weird right now. Listen, it's Sunday, I'm out of here. If you find anything else, let me know. Thanks anyway. Pappas. Wozniak."

Without a trace of hesitation he walked out of the room.

Carl imitated him with a vengeance. "Pappas. Wozniak. Bwuh."

"He's not buying it, Carl."

"I know how to smoke out that Topanga. He knows what happened to Victoria."

"Don't do anything funny, Carl. Phil's outraged. Don't make it worse."

The chair turned round another five times after Carl got up. "Thank you, Don. Maybe I got this all wrong. Switch of your gear, we're moving. There's still a piece of weekend left."

"My mother taught me never to take the last piece."

"Did she now? Then your mother was a tart."

He bent over to avoid an ashtray. He succeeded, but it rained ashes and cigarette butts.

— — —

"You did not hear me say that," sounded the icy voice of the secretary of the Executive Board through the speaker on Carl's desk on the seventeenth floor of WCBN.

"What didn't I hear you say? That he's absent or that he's in a meeting?"

"I said: Mr. Topanga is not available."

"Woman, what the hell does that mean? Is he in the building or not?"

Temperatures were falling. Stupid, Carl thought. Get a hold of yourself, boy, or you'll get absolutely nowhere. If the Polyfe Inc. headquarters had not been a thousand kilometers away he would simply have driven there that very evening. If you're on the spot then you know right away if the man you're looking for is hiding for the media or actually out of office.

"You must understand that a lot of people want to talk to Mr. Topanga. Of course I understand you're with the radio. And so you should know this is my standard response. If I ever say exactly where he is and what he's doing then people put me on the spot immediately. So I have to be vague. Can I make an appointment for you with one of the division directors, Mr. ... Paapes?"

"Páppas. Carl Pappas. Are you aware that Bernard was one of the guests in my radio show a month ago? In The Boardroom? Of WCBN Radio? The show has gotten a bit of a coda. It's urgent."

The voice on the other side might as well have sounded from the refrigeration cell at a butcher's.

"I know precisely who you are, Mr. Paapes."

"Pappas."

"And I'll do my utmost to arrange a telephone meeting for you, with whomever."

"Not with whomever. With Bernard Topanga."

The woman responded evasively. "Can I reach you at this number?"

"Yes," said Carl disappointed. "I'd really appreciate that. If you're not too busy there at Polyfe. What does that name stand for anyway?"

There was a short silence.

She's now wondering if I'm joking her, thought Carl.

"It's a contraction of polypropylene and life," said the woman. "Polyfe Incorporated, you see? Bye Mr. Paapes."

He threw the phone on his desk. Polyfe. Polyfe. What does that bring to mind? Suddenly he knew: pro-life, the anti abortion movement in the United States. But you can't change the name of a multinational that operates on all continents just because there's a few citizens marching in protest. A long time a go he'd had a group of representatives of the movement in his show to debate about doctor George Tiller, who'd been killed because he performed abortions on women in a rather late stage of their pregnancy. The man had been shot in the hall of his own church. That was an episode he'd never forget because it had been one of the pillars of his show's fame through the years.

The day unfolded without serious interruptions. The American stock exchanges continued their upward mobility, the Europeans doubted, the Asians where in the doldrums.

The previous week had ended in a different lineup, one of doubting Americans, Europeans in the doldrums and Asians on the rise. The result was a global croquette in which everything was grinded and wrapped in a crispy layer; a professional investor could not distinguish the different tastes. Anyone who changed positions, like the exchanges, was taking great risks. Because it was impossible to see a pattern; the magic word was "spreading". In the old days there were the time zones, that gave every exchange region a sixteen-hour break a day, roughly. But that was a thing of the past now; somewhere in the night from Sunday to Monday the worldwide exchanges switched to the new week simultaneously and no longer stopped till the night from Friday to Saturday.

This gave him an idea. I have to dedicate a show to people who can get by on incredibly little sleep. What vitamins they're taking. If they're born with it. How the keep up with it as they grow older. The future belongs to the sleepless, Carl thought, there's really no time for sleep with all these exchanges running full time. What progress is science making in the support of business people who no longer wish to sleep, or who sleep no more than four hours in every twenty-four as and when they want?

By the time The Boardroom's Monday night edition was ready for takeoff it was clear to Carl that Bernard Topanga's secretary was not going to return the call. Apparently the man was hiding from him. Fortunately Pappas, being a bizz jockey — or rather: the bizz jockey — controlled a mighty weapon: the radio. With his ten million listeners in the important business cities of the world no one could evade him. So his phone calls were always answered. So no one was in a hurry to refuse an invitation to appear on the show. It was better to suffer the sweat of a live broadcast than run the risk of being condemned in absentia; that's how business circles thought of the program. But with regular intervals someone whose name was mentioned in The Boardroom took up the gauntlet and sued WCBN Radio. Immediately the network's usual lawyer's firm was alarmed and the defense attorneys of Jerome & Wagner appeared. Their regular legal counsel for the affairs of Carl Pappas was Mr. Louis B. Luigi.

Carl got along with Mr. Luigi particularly well. Not because the man was a cunning lawyer who provided him and WCBN Radio with a safety net many times if statements made on the radio threatened to bring them down, and delivered them a safe landing. Legal hairsplittings didn't bother the world's most famous bizz jockey in the least; he was always focused on the big picture, on the vision and the philosophy, on the mainsprings and the morals.

Luigi never beat around the bush and spent little time on pleasantries. He was all courteousness, but only while doing business. That's why a phone call to Luigi was always fruitful (notwithstanding the invoice that would arrive at Phil Solo's, reserving the pleasant aspects of the legal practice for Carl).

"The man's not suing you?" asked Luigi bluntly.

"No," said Carl. "My only question is: how do I get the man to answer the phone? Can you exert some pressure somewhere?"

"Direct as much energy in the shortest possible time

towards the smallest possible target," said Luigi. "You do know Von Clausewitz's war strategies?"

The Von Clausewitz conceptions were part of Louis B. Luigi's standard repertoire.

"Just put some pressure on the most sensible of points, namely the radio. Any other strategy will cost you time and money."

"At your risk, Louis?"

"I'm hanging, Pappas, before you make me laugh. I can't have that in my business. Capiche? Ciao!"

Carl checked the CNN website during the last seconds before the broadcast. His suspicions were confirmed: the disappearance of Rosa Colombina, also known as Victoria, was gaining news value.

"I can héar her six-pack," said Don Wozniak.

And damned if it wasn't true entered Hitomi.

Suddenly from the studio speakers, thanks to Don's magic hand, sounded Rod Stewart's "Passion". This was Wozniak's favorite running gag, which he had kept going for a couple of years now. Hitomi ignored Don entirely and exchanged a glance of mutual understanding with Carl Pappas. Her natural, oriental modesty and softness surfaced for a moment, as if she actually knew something resembling shyness, she removed some hair from her face while looking at him from the corner of her eyes.

"I prefer 'Da Ya Think I'm Sexy?' by Rod Stewart," she then yelled. Her voice snarled through the room. "But of course he doesn't dare to put that one on because obviously he knows the answer to that."

"Bitch," said Don, but he mumbled with such softness that no one heard.

Hitomi strode past him towards the studio. Why don't we kick him out so I don't have to take the guests through that incredible rathole time and again, she thought. But she never complained about it, because some clean, neat, young, fresh, athletic sound engineer also has its dangers, if you're a hardworking single.

Seven

The "On the Air" lamp lit up. From that moment on the airwaves and the internet were filled with Carl Pappas' show.

The tune sounded. The mysterious, deep voice of WCBN, whose owner was known only to Carl, thundered the announcement: "It's eleven o'clock. The city is dark, but the fire burns. It burns in the offices. It burns on Wall Street. It burns in the City. It burns on the Bund. It burns in Dubai. It burns in the factories and power plants. And it burns within us. Because we are the business and we all need redemption. This is the hour of delusion and today's truth. This is The Boardroom. Here is your prophet, the buddy and the bodyguard of every CEO, the Don Juan of every business babe. Here is the world's one and only bizz jockey. Here is your BJ: Carl Pappas!"

Carl put his teeth in it.

"Annnd... it's Monday night. If you haven't scored yet now it's time to ask yourself how you're going to get through the remainder of the week. For some of us the day is done, for others the clock just goes on ticking. But this is the moment to realize: the die is cast. So what will it be this week: stand up straight or feel the whip? Monday always makes me think of this CFO who goes to the store to buy a new calculator with a built in printer. The sales guy says: 'We don't sell calculators like that anymore. These days everybody has a calculator on his laptop and an app on his smartphone, so there's no demand.' But the CFO won't take no for an answer. He says: 'I want one of those classic calculators with a roll on top so everything I calculate is actually printed on that roll.' The sales guy totally doesn't get it, he says: 'But there's no need for that anymore, there's software for your computer that keeps the score.' Says the CFO: 'I don't give a damn, I'm just used to my boss coming in and wiping his ass with my numbers.'"

Carl illustrated the last sentence by raising his hand and gesturing with his index finger; enough for Don Wozniak to start a new tune, a kind of drumroll backed up by three singers that sang "WCBN Radiooo".

"What kind of week will this be? And I'm not asking the weatherman, I'm asking you: the international business community. I can give you a hint though. A question that must be answered this week is of course: 'Where is Victoria'. For those of you that've missed it: the broadcast that had Victoria as guest is available for listening on our website. She was reported missing this weekend. Look, people, there's been scolding in that broadcast, so there's plenty of suspect characters, but in the tumultuous history of The Boardroom this is the premiere of the disappearance of a guest. So the question is: does it have anything to do with our show or nothing at all? You can call us after our next item. I also invite Bernard Topanga and Olof Stockholm to call. They were present. What do they think of the disappearance of Victoria, after she revealed the existence of an exclusive network of call girls for chief executive officers? Let's have another listen to the responses of Bernard Topanga to Victoria's revelations!"

Carl's finger rose into the air and Don started the soundbite.

"The lady would be wise to pay a little more attention to what she's saying before accidents start to happen."

"Accidents, Bernard? Are you threatening Victoria?"

"No. No, but..."

"But what?"

"Madame can not simply throw mud at a professional group. It is called slander and these are not the kind of people who will condone that."

"Should she call her lawyer? Is that what you're saying?"

"Or worse."

Carl gestured that the fragment had to stop and took over again. "I'm just saying, people, hard words have been said. Am I the only one here who's wondering what exactly Bernard Topanga's point was? Doesn't it sound suspiciously like... a threat?"

From behind the glass Hitomi made the "telephone" gesture.

"But first we'll be talking to Lola Mercalina about a problem that's coming our way: the growth of alternative currency Civil, used among civilians to trade services. Following the American IRS now China wants to tax this giant black currency too. Lola, it's so unfortunate this is not TV. What are you wearing?"

Phil Solo eyed the studio from behind the glass. As usual the famous bizz jockey was oblivious to anybody standing behind the visitor's window. The only eye contact possible, as long as the "On the Air" lamp was on, was with Don Wozniak and Hitomi Sakamoto. That gave Phil the opportunity to look on undisturbed, which obviously had little meaning. He might as well listen in his office or in his car. One could say many things about Solo, but he always listened to the show because it was thé great crowd-pleaser of WCBN Radio. Carl Pappas was the only disk jockey of the radio station that had the full attention of the management. Not that they were left with much choice: on a regular basis the other networks and newspapers furiously jumped on WCBN the day after a broadcast of The Boardroom and Phil didn't like being taken by surprise.

He beckoned Hitomi.

"Call Mr. Luigi," he said.

"Tomorrow?" asked Hitomi.

"Tomorrow? Do I look like Nostradamus? Nów, Sakamoto."

Eight

They were watching the flatscreen opposite Phil Solo's desk, which flashed the CNN brunette. Judging from her widespread eyes something of the utmost importance had happened in the world. Even her blinding smile had been suppressed as much as possible. But her appearance still clashed with the drama that unfolded before their very eyes; she was beautiful enough to be a fashion model, dressed in haute couture, her face symmetrical, perfectly straight and white teeth and nice, long hands that moved elegantly across the table — but the topic at hand showed the world at its ugliest.

"The affair of the woman known as the 'CEO Groupie', owner of a supposed network of expensive call girls and gigolos for top executives, has now claimed a second victim. After the disappearance of Victoria, the CEO Groupie, it now seems to be Bernard Topanga's turn. The chairman of Polyfe Inc. was one of her fellow guests in bizz jockey Carl Pappas' radio show The Boardroom. The stocks of Polyfe Inc. are currently making a nosedive, an apparent consequence of statements made by Topanga in The Boardroom."

Louis Luigi looked straight at the screen.

Phil Solo looked straight out the window.

Carl Pappas leaned back in one of the fauteuils and said: "Damn! She's hot. Even my girlfriend will admit to that and she's real picky."

"Pappas, be serious for a moment, we have to come up with a strategy here."

"If the apocalypse begins, and I mean the real thing, she's going to have to break the bad news. It's the only way to prevent a worldwide panic."

Solo zapped off the screen with the remote. "You're ruining that Topanga, Carl. And all that for something stupid he said in your show. I mean: what did he say? He said she had to be careful about what she said. That's what he said. Big deal. Louis?"

"There's a subpoena already," said Louis with his unmistakable Southern European accent.

Carl mumbled a curse.

"So what's the litigation?" asked Phil.

"Immediate discontinuation of announcements that suggest a connection between Polyfe and Bernard Topanga on the one hand, and the disappearance of Victoria on the other. Additionally there may be a claim for damages."

Carl made a clacking sound with his tongue.

Phil reacted with irritation, blowing up his cheeks like balloons and hissing through his teeth. "You must realize that Topanga's reputation has been compromised áfter Carl made the connection during his show. Not a single other news source has done that earlier."

"Freedom of information?" tried Carl.

"We'll certainly try that and it's also reasonably watertight, but unfortunately, and annoying at that, your reporting is incredibly suggestive, Carl. That wouldn't cause problems had it stopped right there, but the investors have taken your word for it. If this goes on Polyfe and Bernard Topanga will be the stock market's Chernobyl before the end of the week. A dead zone. If they can prove that this was caused directly by Carl's statements, then we have to prove it's freedom of information and not just some jerk-off kicking from a position of power."

"A position of power?" said Carl. He jumped up, roaring through his nostrils.

"When you have ten million listeners you are in a position of power, end of line," said Louis.

"Not that argument again, Pappas," added Phil Solo. "You want nothing to do with it, fine. But let me hammer it into your thick skull: yes, you have a position of power. That is not an opinion, it is a fact."

"It is even a legal fact," said Louis Luigi smiling.

"You are so full of shit," said Carl aloud. "Victoria has disappeared without a trace. I'm only concerned about her resurfacing. I thought Topanga behaved suspiciously and all I said was: call me on the show. That is what I'll tell the judge: I called him, I was fobbed off. Nicely by the book. If you ask me it'll be a shorty in court. Piece of cake."

Luigi smiled from ear to ear.

Solo mumbled a curse. "So far you're right. But from here on it becomes a delicate thing. Now it's becoming clear that the public's opinion is turning against Topanga and Polyfe Inc. and the damage done is becoming formidable it's time for you to rise above all doubts. Ignore the whole thing in your show from now on. Or else they'll blame you for inflaming public opinion. You don't need that. Agree?"

"Agree," said Mr. Luigi.

"Fine," said Carl. He walked out of the room and yelled behind him: "That's a deal then. You guys can handle it from here?"

Although the ashtray had once again been removed, Don Wozniak's shack smelled stale. The odor that betrays the hardened outdoor smoker; the smoker that longs back to his younger days, long before the anti-smoking laws, but can't put himself to leaving those times behind. Even a non-smoker prefers the smell of a fresh cigarette or cigar to the staleness that emanates from the clothes and the hair of the outdoor smoker, the portico puffer, the sideway junkie. Fortunately for Don Wozniak this place didn't always smell like this. It would certainly attract some officious WCBN Radio paper pusher to kick him into therapy or discharge.

Don Wozniak had a strong distaste for both.

Carl came in, worried, hurried by the nervous voice of his sound engineer and assistant.

"What's up Don?"

The man immediately erupted into a coughing fit. It wasn't until his boss patted him firmly on the shoulders that he could talk again.

"Do you remember the guy you got on the phone, live, shortly after Victoria's disappearance was announced?"

"Yes. I don't remember exactly what he said. Calamity Caller."

Calamity Caller was the usual denomination for callers in the show that were attracted by the suffering of others. If one of Carl's guests had caused the evaporation of pension fund billions or lost a lawsuit or carried the responsibility for an oil spill disaster, you could be sure the next caller would be a Calamity Caller.

"I could not leave it alone. I brought in the recording. A friend of mine has software that allows you to compare voices and let the computer calculate the percentage by which they're similar."

"To what voice do you want to compare this Calamity Caller?"

"Just listen."

Don hit a button. Through the speakers Carl heard himself in the role of bizz jockey, the world's most successful BJ.

"Here's John from London. Go ahead John."

"Give up the search for Victoria," said a subdued voice.

"Wow, we have an insider on the phone. Are we talking about the same Victoria, John?"

"She doesn't want to be in the media anymore and is tired of the business," whispered the caller.

"What's with the conspiracy act, John. You sound like you're talking through a handkerchief. Do you know where she is?"

"It is over for Victoria. I took care of that myself. It had to be done. She deserved it. She's not coming back and there's no need to look for her."

The connection was terminated.

"Does that go for the investigators too, John? Because they're looking harder than I am. People, I tell you: the Lord has some strange boarders, and some of them are calling The Boardroom."

Don Wozniak switched of the recording. "This voice I ran through the computer, together with a couple of others. Like this one."

Again he pushed a button and started a soundbite. Carl sat down in one of the desk chairs, leaned with his elbows on Don's panel and folded his hands under his chin.

"I run a conglomerate of companies, that all together deal in everything from raw materials to end product."

As if hit in the face by a woman Pappas veered up. "Olof Stockholm? You have got to be joking."

"The computer says their voices match for ninety-four percent."

"How reliable is that? I don't hear any resemblance."

"It seems he did an amazing job twisting his voice. But you can rely on this, it's software also used by the secret services of the US, Britain, France, Israel, China, Russia..."

"Oh, so the KGB uses it too."

"The KGB was terminated, Carl. What will you do now?"

There was no answer.

The clicking of a cigarette lighter, puffing sounds. Don Wozniak thought for a moment and said: "You're not going to do anything weird, are you? What do we tell ten million listeners if something happens to you?"

"The show must go on, Don. You know how I feel about that," said Carl Pappas grimly. He looked at the clock. "We got some broadcasting to do. So much the better. Means I can sit on it for a while."

Nine

Even if you're the most successful — or at least the only — bizz jockey, you'll still have your occasional off day. There will still be times when you just don't feel the urge. Carl Pappas thoughts were elsewhere, but that didn't stop him from doing the broadcast full throttle. That was also one of the reasons of his success: he never failed to deliver.

Surely he had his own methods to get himself on track. The best method was the joke. Especially if he made them up on the spot; that boosted the adrenaline and by itself brought him into the right mood. Call it a natural stimulant.

"Here is your prophet, the buddy and the bodyguard of every CEO, the Don Juan of every business babe. Here is the world's one and only bizz jockey. Here is your BJ: Carl Pappas!"

"Huh humm," coughed Carl. "I know you all think I'm a joker. But I am dead serious. Am I dead serious, Don?"

The sound engineer responded immediately, as if previously agreed. "About as mortal as it gets, Carl."

"You have his word of honor, people. Keep that in mind during the following story. So I'm checking in at the Valdofas

Doria Hotel. Not for fun, but because I have to do some business too; I have to make preparations for this show and talk to people, also sometimes I have to play the clown before the board of directors of WCBN Radio and their associates during dinners and stuff, you know what I'm talking about. Anyway, I'm checking in. Next to me stands a straight business suit, a BE, a business empress, what shall I call it: a woman of seniority, of radiance. Behind her stand three men, sort of the same age, they're carrying suitcases that can only be hers. She looks to her side. I say: 'Good morning.' She says: 'I hope so for you.' Look, there's my kind of lady. Anyway, it's not her turn right away and what's worse: she's being skipped by the receptionist to deal with another guest first. It is so blatantly obvious, I would have blown. But she doesn't move a muscle. She just takes her cell phone and starts making a call. I cannot hear precisely what's she's saying. Right before it's finally her turn, she suddenly starts talking louder. What I hear is: 'Did you buy it? Good. The first thing that needs to be done is to...' She looks at the name tag on the receptionist's jacket and says: '...is to dismiss Robert Falliago immediately.' So everybody's standing there as if struck by lightning. People look at each other a bit silly. Then the manager comes in through a door behind the reception. He whispers something in the receptionist's ear, who pales and disappears through the door. Next thing the lady's served by the manager with the utmost urgency. All I'm saying, people, is: business is business. May I have the first caller?"

"Rosario Ulmarov."

"Well, you've just scored points with the most original name for starters, though a little strange also. Brazilian mother and Russian father?"

"None of your business, Pappas. Say, wasn't that a bit patriarchal, what you just told us? As soon as a woman is rich and powerful she starts acting dumb and throw money?"

"Listen Rosario, I'm not responsible, I'm just telling you what happened."

"Then get the manager of the, what's the hotel's name, and have him confirm your story. Such rubbish, it is a joke and a sexist one too, that's the point."

"The only sexist here is you, Ulmarov. I am always telling jokes starring male managers and I never hear you complain once. Then the only time I put a woman in..."

"Ah! So you admit it was a joke and didn't really take place!"

"Bye, Ulmarov."

A dry click sounded.

"A caller's end always sounds a bit like the cocking of a pistol," sighed Carl, deep into the microphone.

— — —

The metropolises of the world have become identical. They all harbor the same predictable neighborhoods full of glass skyscrapers (the financial district), aged warehouses and housing blocks (where the artists live and work), villas (where the old money lives, but also the rock stars, super models and criminals), condominiums and terraced houses (the middle and upper middle classes) and the neglected social housing projects (if there are no slums) and shacks (for the poorest). But among all that uniformity there's always this rare building that thoroughly clashes with its surroundings and actually has a unique quality.

The central police station was located only two blocks from WCBN Radio. The skyscrapers that filled the streets in between could have stood anywhere in the world: Toronto, Shanghai, Rio de Janeiro, London, Berlin, Mumbai. They were isomorphous glass needles, standing neatly in line, mirrored in the river that cut the city in half. Carl rushed over the broad but empty sidewalk. If you wake up one day, he thought, and find yourself standing on a crossroads of two avenues with skyscrapers, and there is no man in sight, then there's no way you can orientate. There was a time when you could say: this is Times Square so I'm in New York. But that is a long time ago. Now it doesn't matter where you are anymore. It could be anyplace.

But when the central police station came into view Carl changed his mind. No, this building can stand nowhere but here, he thought. Boy, did this pile of bricks stick out like a sore thumb! It was horribly at odds with the glass and steel and concrete of the surrounding buildings. The loud yellow bricks, presumably backed especially for this purpose to meet the architect's demands, clashed with the modest gray and blue of glass, steel and concrete. The fiery red windowsills and the bars screamed. The fifty steps stairway looked so primitive compared to the glass sliding doors of the neighbors. He stumbled three times; it appeared that the distance between the steps was not right for a man of average height. The revolving doors were a constant cause of animosity between people wanting to go in and those who wanted to leave, because they had no prefixed turning direction. Next you entered the acoustic nightmare called "main hall". To the left was an endless counter with rows of people in the front of it, either having loud arguments with the police officials on duty or with each other. To the right were dozens of benches where hundreds of people were waiting; some used the premises for purposes to which it was not intended and slept unashamed. Opposite the revolving doors stood the detection gates, waiting for all visitors that had been sent through from the counter. There were cabins with curtains, allowing the occasional thorough strip search. For some reason the floor (marble), walls (bricks) and the domed ceiling (too high to see what it was made of) created a horrible echo of every single noise. Everything from shoe shuffling to suicide bombing was endlessly repeated and mixed.

Carl looked at the rows and decided to address an officer posted near the revolving doors.

"I've an emergency for lieutenant Carlsberg," he said. "I'm with WCBN Radio."

The man looked at him unmoved. "You can stand in line over there, sir," he said dryly.

"Carl Pappas, WCBN Radio. I have a clue in an important missing person case that even keeps the mayor awake at night."

"Will you please remain calm, sir, and stand in line? Nice and proper, like everyone else."

Carl inhaled, deep.

An hour later he cursed in Carlsberg's office. The man was not impressed.

"Don't get yourself all worked up, Pappas. Anyway, you're precisely too late. Listen, I got Bernard Topanga sitting in the room next door. While I'm on it I get a call from above telling me to release him immediately and that's what I'm going to do now. This Victoria gets around in high society and I'm not going to get my fingers burned."

"Now wait a minute... Bernard Topanga is sitting in the room next door?"

"Yes. And I am going to kick him out along with you. My boss is going to love it: efficiency."

Carl sighed. "OK. I admit: Topanga is innocent. But I got some new information; my sound engineer had some voices compared by a computer. I mean: we're talking top-notch software from intelligence services. It's Olof Stockholm you should be..."

But the lieutenant raised his hand, his index finger piercing the air to silence Carl and walked to the door. "Intelligence service software. Nice going, Pappas. I'll pretend I didn't hear that. And you leave this Stockholm guy in one piece, because thanks to your behavior I'm already getting my ass kicked from upstairs."

It was quiet in the Gulag. Even Katie kept a low profile. Perhaps she saw the serious faces of Carl and Bernard as they entered and sat down silently at one of the tables. She didn't even take orders but brought strong coffee without being asked. That's the way of the Gulag.

"Why would someone like Olof Stockholm make an anonymous phone call and rant such psychopathic lines? Also he didn't seem extraordinarily interested in Victoria, if I remember correctly. I was the one who got angry, remember?"

"Jesus, Topanga."

"Do you really have to do that, curse?"

"I never curse when I'm on the air. Listen, it sounds farfetched to me too. But what if we assume the anonymous caller's voice is his."

"Call him up and ask him."

"Just go along with it. Will you. At least as long as you're taking the time to drink that coffee."

"In that case you can take it easy. This coffee is undrinkable, so that's going to take a while."

They looked at each other a moment.

"I was wrong about you and what's worse, I voiced that in my show. I've blackened you."

"Would you please write that down and sign it? That's exactly what my lawyers need. Man, if they find out I'm sitting here talking to you..."

Bernard Topanga turned to where Katie was standing to ask for the check.

"We have to expect nothing from the police and from lawyers," Carl rushed to say. "The damage to your reputation means nothing to them. Hell, that lieutenant Carlsberg interrupted me at 'Olof'. I never even got to 'Stockholm'. That's why we have to take action ourselves."

"We?"

"Yes. How do we get near to Stockholm?"

They looked at each other again. Neither of them blinked.

"No jokes about Sweden now, please," said Pappas. "I've made a few attempts, but there's no way to find out where he is at the moment. He's as good a master at hiding himself as you are, Topanga."

"It's a necessary evil."

"We could go to his house."

"Not good enough. He probably has an extra house or apartment where he can hide her."

"The man has houses here and there. Barcelona. Chesapeake. Hong Kong. He's also Sean Connery's neighbor in Greece, Madonna's in...'

"Yeah sure," muttered Carl. "Never mind. This is a dead end. I'm bringing in just the man for the job." He gestured Katie, who responded immediately. "Do that to me one more time, honey. And add the check to it." And to Bernard Topanga: "You have no idea what some guys can find out on the internet for you in one hour."

Ten

"Do you know the story of the man who worked in a chip shop and claimed he was Elvis?"

Carl sat on the steel bench in the park along the riverbank, his back to the WCBN Radio building. In his mind he cursed the imprints the cold iron made on his buttocks and his back. He had forgotten how long-winded Mach One could be. The man who got his alias from his ability to gather information super-fast, people who had disappeared, hidden contacts, secret companies in tax havens in far away subtropical regions and, if necessary, ultimately, with satellite photos of silhouettes on swimming pool edges. So he was full of stories, but he also took the time for it. Because one did not interrupt Ross York, alias Mach One. Carl had done that once and immediately found himself waving goodbye to his information; but that had perhaps been because he was the only non-paying customer. Ross York considered it an honor to collaborate with The Boardroom, but he had his limits. He had mentioned his name once to Carl, years ago, when they made their acquaintances. "Never call me that," he had said. "It can be dangerous. Some Russian godfathers hate my guts.

Hell, even some guys from NASA."

So Mach One it was and so Carl, shivering, listened to the story of the guy who worked in a chip shop and claimed he was Elvis. Ah, Elvis, thought Carl. Those were the days. But the story was good and it made him laugh and he realized he would repeat it one day live on The Boardroom.

"Were you an Elvis fan, Mach?" he asked, to keep the spirit up.

"Absolutely," rasped Mach One, bringing out a cigarette and lighting it. "'You Ain't Nothin' But a Hound Dog'! My father used to play that in the car, a Silver Thunderbird, real loud, and we'd cruise Main Street and all the girls and women would look. Mom would OK that, you have to grant your man some fun, she used to say. My favorite was 'Return to Sender', that one really gave me the urge."

Mach One really looked like a Cold War spy. He had hidden his tall body underneath a dark raincoat, wore a sloppy hat and dark sunglasses on his nose. That nose was quite the sight, it showed he'd taken some beatings in his time, a tough one, underlined by thick, protruding lips and vertical scar on the upper lip, leaving only two-thirds of space for his moustache to fully grow. He was a nervous man, with dandruff on his dark raincoat, and he continuously tapped his foot to a rhythm — possible from an Elvis song.

Just as fast as his stories started pouring out of him as they said hello, they ebbed away. He pulled his hat from his head, took off his glasses and turned to Pappas. "Powerful man. He's not what he seems. Look, you think: a multinational's good CEO. Maybe a little too wealthy. But his influence stretches as far as the White House. Downing Street. The Elysee.

Tiananmen Square."

"Criminal?"

"In what kind of world do you live? No, the man is clean. Unless you're inclined to believing the super rich use too much of their influence to become even richer." A rasp followed, a sputum, a coughing fit.

"Politics don't do you any good, Mach," said Carl sarcastically.

"No," laughed Mach One. "One day it'll be the death of me. It's a good thing you're getting this information just like that, simply because you are the bizz jockey. He's at the Great Lake in one of his villas. He's doing his business from there, he leaves there and returns there, but he's very inconspicuous about that. Dark car, travels at night, does his boarding under another name. He's making every effort, because the house is just a one hour flight from his headquarters and his staff leave him alone when he's there."

"Does he have guests there?"

"There's one guest with an unknown cell phone number. They call each other. There's also security, but they're the regular guys. The guest's cell phone number has only been in use at that location for the past two weeks and never anywhere else. Possibly someone who's hiding there."

A helicopter and its mirror image rushed across the silent water of the river. Mach One looked at it and inhaled deeply. He rubbed his chin and made smacking sounds as if he longed for coffee. Carl Pappas stared at the helicopter as it flew away. His thoughts ran off to Victoria and Olof Stockholm and when he was startled and hurled back and looked to his side, Mach

One had disappeared. He smiled. To think he had planned to deny the man any opportunity to run off without saying goodbye this time.

Mach One had once again proven his reputation.

"New money," said Bernard Topanga, with revilement, as they moved through the hills, following the winding road around the Great Lake. Here stood the great villas, separated by giant gardens and insurmountable walls. Topanga's Jaguar crossed the road silently and Carl had time to think about this characterization. How does one tell if a house is paid for with new money and not with an ancient family fortune? Most houses had stood here for many years, the walls around the premises buried under heavy ivy, the house itself hiding behind the grove.

"Your money ain't old?" asked Carl after a while.

"All I did was look after my parents assets and prolong it." The CEO looked dark. "Right now the value of my family's property is considerably lower compared to when my parents left it to my brothers and me. Thanks to you."

"Don't whine, Topanga," snarled Pappas. "You're part of an economic system we call capitalism in which money is not deterred by anything. I refuse to participate in the dictatorship of stock exchange compliance, that backroom nonsense. Has the CEO developed a heart condition? Don't tell, because it is bad for the stock value. Is he suffering from chronic fatigue? Don't tell. You people are doing it to yourselves; your whole lives are chained to the anonymous stock exchange index. No one feels any responsibility; in the mean time you're pointing your finger at outsiders."

Carl sighed. "We're not even broadcasting. Too bad. I was really on a roll here."

"Stockholm's house is just around that corner."

"We'd better park here then. We can't likely ring the bell. Perhaps there's a way to get to the house down there at the lakeshore."

Topanga turned the car to a small parking lot, which marked the beginning of a path down towards to the lake. He switched off the engine.

"Why don't we do precisely that? I ring and distract him. Do you think you can climb across his fence just like that? Surely he has an alarm system."

"Dogs? Security?"

"I've no idea."

"Come on, Topanga. Be creative for a change. You got the connections and the money and the means and the power to put us down right into that garden in a jiffy. Don't you have some nice polypropylene trampoline or a hang glider from one of your factories?"

"I'm sure I do," muttered Bernard. "I'll call my helicopter pilot. That'll speed things up."

"Your helicopter pilot. Good idea."

"Stupid idea, Pappas. We'll simply ring the doorbell. What are you thinking: he won't let us in? If he is home and I call my name, or yours, he won't fob us off. You can take my word for it. You just have to be sure he's home right now."

An hour earlier Mach One had texted a message saying that Olof Stockholm had arrived at his country home at the Great Lake on Friday night. It was Saturday night now. Everything was going according to plan.

In the end Bernard was proven right. The wrought iron gate in the wall surrounding Olof Stockholm's estate swung open right after he had yelled "Bernard Topanga" in the intercom. They drove across the driveway through an ocean of rhododendrons, lit from the ground by a chain of lights along the gravel, and saw a villa appear. Two men in dark suits awaited them and escorted them to the house, through the front door into the main hall. There stood Olof Stockholm in a shining duster, his hands filled with a cigar and a glass of wine. It appeared he was unmoved by the sudden appearance of the visitors. "Come," he said. "You're my guests."

He preceded them into a living room, that seemed to go on without an end. To the right the room disappeared around corners and behind panels and closets and a floating fireplace, to the left there was nothing but glass looking out on the Great Lake, way down. From the speakers WCBN Radio sounded, featuring one of many other programs about international business.

"What are you guys having?" asked Stockholm, who had moved into a design kitchenette, beyond a short bar furnished with three stools and booze and a coffee machine.

Carl slammed his flat hand on the bar. "Nothing. You want me to chat away, lurking a cigar and some whiskey, while there's some serious trouble going on?"

Topanga gave the bizz jockey a little push. He gestured vaguely with his hand. In the half-light of a corridor that bent away beyond a brick chimney they saw Victoria. She stood there, silently, but said nothing. Like Stockholm, she was dressed in a duster and had apparently washed her exhaustive hair recently; it had been pinned up and was hiding underneath a towel draped in the shape of a turban. She nodded affably and disappeared.

"Victoria!" shouted Carl. He ran into the corridor.

Behind him the two CEOs started to argue.

After a few corners the bizz jockey caught up with the woman. He grabbed her elbow and turned her around. They were standing in the doorway of a bedroom.

"Victoria," panted Carl. "You are... all right?"

"What do you think?" said Victoria.

"There's people all around worrying about you, Victoria. Why are you hiding? Or is he keeping you here?"

"Of course not, Carl. Listen, go and sit by the fireplace. I'll get dressed and join you. OK? And don't be angry with Olof, he wanted to protect me."

"Protect you? Against whom?"

"From the real stalker," said Olof Stockholm.

They had settled themselves by the fireplace, which had been lit shortly before. The logs were fresh and crackled enthusiastically. The sun had now gone down entirely. In the distance the lights of other villas along the lake's shore were shining. Carl looked at the scenery and thought it utterly boring; a cliché a man his age knows from a thousand postcards and movies.

"Immediately after the broadcast someone started stalking me," said Victoria. "It was serious. He got to me everywhere, at my work, at home, he succeeded in retrieving my every secret phone number or e-mail address."

They saw one of Stockholm's men pass outside the window,

looking out across the lake. Not everybody hates clichés.

"That's why I offered to hide her here," said Olof.

"We had stayed in touch after the broadcast," said Victoria.

"For business?" asked Bernard Topanga sarcastically.

His sarcasm makes sense, thought Carl. After all he's the whole affair's number one victim. But he didn't say. "Why did you make an anonymous phone call to my show to talk nonsense?"

"I was hoping to discourage the real stalker."

"And did you succeed?" asked Carl.

"It looks like it," said Victoria. "My new secret phone number has not been called by him for two weeks now and he's no longer in my e-mail box. He's not bothering my office anymore either."

"Nice good news show we're having here," said Carl. "All's well that ends well and stuff. But I still find it hard to believe that such a stalker can be put off so easily."

"Someone in a position like Victoria's will always be bothered by weird little men," grinned Stockholm. "As soon as they find that they're not dealing with a woman alone, they're gone. And she's also safe with me because I got round the clock security as it is, wherever I go." He looked at Victoria. "We mean to make that more permanent. We're getting married."

"And you're quitting the business," said Carl, a man who had an eye for the unpredictability of life.

But no one responded to that. Bernard Topanga suddenly did cough very loud though. It was a high-pitched, nervous sound, something between a cough and a hiccup. They all turned heads and looked at him. He looked back. When no one said anything, he coughed again.

"You wanted to say something, Topanga?"

The CEO coughed again. His face went sour and he stared ominously at Olof Stockholm.

Eleven

Whenever you mix business with women things start to go wrong, thought Carl Pappas. Like clockwork. And what better time for looking at the clock than the early moments of dusk, with the rained city lying wrung out and shining in the light of the office buildings, where there's still people working on overtime or on adultery?

He stood there musing semi-poetically, while the hour of his radio show approached with the speed of a taxi, driven by a chauffeur who's looking forward to a five hundred dollar tip if he puts the pedal to the metal. Pappas listened to the voice of his conscience with growing disgust. The conscience spoke with the sultry voice of a mistress with a hidden agenda, to begin with. Which didn't imply that he listened closely, because whatever his conscience was telling him was hard to swallow, whether you had the mouth of a whale or the stomach of a mouse. "Don't start it," she seemed to be saying. "Women and business are trouble."

Carl shook it all off him while he looked down seventeen floors, to the headlights of the cars in the deep, flickering like strings of Christmas lights. Is it an obsession of mine, he wondered, to always shock or insult guests in order to bring my message across? Do I have to be looking for a fight for the rest of my life? The hassle is part of the job. It's good for the ratings, but by now you should've learned not to interfere with the love life of people in high society. Too many skeletons in the closet. Elegant people, but still skeletons.

Pappas shrugged. His internal air conditioner (built into his chest at the approximate height of his heart) kick started and ice water began to flow through his veins. Right on time, as usual every working day: a cold man live on the air. He turned his back to the city and strode out of his office, through the corridor, passing the framed advertising posters and the prize cabinet with the dozens of bronze, silver and gold statuettes and plaques, and the coffee machines and the abandoned counter, around the corner, through the door to the shack of sound engineer Don Wozniak.

Who was ready to seriously show off today.

"He is *the man* and he is once again putting his money where his mouth is. It's the one and only bizz jockey, your BJ Carl Pappas and... it's the man himself. It is time for... the hour of truth."

"Thank you Don."

"Had a good weekend?"

"Go wash your mouth with soap, Wozniak."

Pappas rubbed his hands as if to invoke static electricity. "Seen Hitomi yet? We got a couple of killer topics today, boy. She arranged some fine stuff for the show."

"Junkies you are," said Carl Pappas. "All of you."

The "On the Air" lamp was lit. Don Wozniak was sitting

there, leaning backwards comfortably, his hand in place for tunes and sound fragments. Hitomi Sakamoto was nosing around in her papers, overlooking the program, but also thinking about future shows that needed preparations, meetings she had to go through, difficult radio announcers that needed to be put in line.

"You are good news junkies. And you're not getting enough of it. CEO, CFO, CMO, chairman or chairwoman, shareholder, investor, young talents: you always get your daily dose of bad news, but who sees to it that you are ready for the battle again, who gives you your daily vitamins in this economic winter? It's your own Carl Pappas, the one and only real bizz jockey. And I tell you from The Boardroom: there is hope yet. Do you remember my guest Bernard Topanga? Yes you remember him: the man who was plagued by suspicions ever since that show. Here in The Boardroom I personally addressed him for the disappearance of Victoria. As he went down he brought the stock value of his own Polyfe Inc. down with him. People, I got good news: he was bailed out by his buddy, his mate Olof Stockholm. Through his own holding Stockholm has brought out an offer on all Polyfe shares. An offer that lies on the level befóre the shares dropped last week. So both Polyfe Inc. and its chairman Bernard Topanga have been rescued from total perdition. Today Victoria is my guest once again; she has done away with her business and will tell us about her new life as first lady of Olof Stockholm. People, there is hope for each of us. We may all be in the gutter, said Oscar Wilde, but you can always look up at the stars. He didn't literally say so, but that doesn't matter, because the rights to his work expired a long, long time ago."

"Hello Mr. Pappas," said Victoria from the other side of the table.

"How are you now, Victoria? How does married life suit you?"

"Extremely well," said Victoria. After all these years of hard labor I enjoy a little resting immensely."

"And love."

"And love, but that goes without saying, Mr. Pappas."

Carl's voice betrayed irritation. Did the remoteness of 'Mr.' annoy him?

"Oh? Does that go without saying, Victoria? I for one don't think it's that logical at all. Love is always defeated first."

"Don't be cynical, Mr. Pappas."

"What's so cynical about that? You're the one who supplied married men and women with paid love for twenty-five years. You don't strike me as someone who believes in real love."

Victoria looked around nervously, to the faces of Hitomi and Don beyond the glass, and other team members. Was Carl Pappas after all, in the end, her wolf in sheep's clothes?

"I believe in love, it just took me a long time finding him."

"What strikes me as odd is that you simply called me Carl the last time you were here and now you call me Mr. Pappas. That's telling, wouldn't you say?"

"I don't remember."

"I do. But who cares. The question is why have you sold your business, Victoria. Why have you gotten rid of your thriving escort service for CEOs? Just because of a few threats?"

"They were serious threats, Pappas." She clearly started to sweat, her makeup could not hide that.

"A woman in your position can get protection. You don't have to get married for that, and even then: you don't have to get rid of your business for something like that."

"Are you calling me a liar, Mr. Pappas?"

Carl inhaled hard, gestured to Don.

With a solid coolness he said: "I wouldn't dare to, Victoria. But I will get back to it, right after these messages from our sponsors."

A commercial block was started.

"Dammit Victoria," snarled Carl outside the hearing of the audience. "You're talking yourself into a corner. Are you calling me a liar: what kind of line is that? What do you expect me to say in response?"

"I expect you to say no."

"Give me a break, Victoria. Your escort organization has vanished from the earth. The whole kit and caboodle is once again, just like it was before, complete invisible. Who's behind it? Who's forced you to sell out so they can dive below the radar? Again?"

Victoria smiled, but a winter frost appeared to trek across her face. "Is that what you want of me, Carl?"

"See? This whole 'Mr. Pappas' stuff is all playacting. You don't mean that in the least."

"I could hardly confess to that sort of stuff during a live broadcast, what's gotten into you. Silly DJ."

"That's still BJ. Bízz jockey. Listen, I'm not some slime, I can't be mister nice guy during the show, as soon as we are on the air I attack. I can't help that. But I don't want to do this to you. I'd rather do it without you then. You'd better go. I'll say... you became indisposed or something."

Beyond the window Hitomi, who could hear the conversation, threw her arms in the air in despair. Don Wozniak looked up from a stack of cassettes and CDs he was working on, his face expressing total bewilderment.

"You are a predator, Carl," said Victoria. "You wanted to publicly rip me to shreds and now you've lost the nerve?" Then she whispered, beyond the ears of even Hitomi and Don: "But I'm glad you're warning me. There are... powerful people behind this, I don't want to provoke them a second time."

She got up from her chair. Did a tear sparkle in her eye? The radio studio lights refused to reveal the answer.

"It was very naive of me to come here again. What was I thinking? What was I thinking of you?"

She walked out of the studio.

"Carl Evangelos Pappas! WHAT THE HELL ARE YOU DOING!" heralded Hitomi through the studio. "What will you be doing the rest of the show? You donkey!"

"Get me Norbert Olsson on the phone. We'll do some live investigative reporting. That'll do."

"But she knows exactly what's going on and you let her walk," screamed Hitomi in one of her rare fits of anger. "After all the trouble we went through!"

Carl shook his head and smiled. Hitomi was right of course. But someone had to draw the line somewhere. What would be the point in publicly putting pressure on Victoria alias Rosa Colombina? She was merely a pawn on the chessboard of corporate lust. Insignificant enough to let her walk. He straightened his back. He smelled prey.

While Carl Pappas drew the microphone closer to him, in the distance, outside the studio, beyond the BJ's hearing, the elevator signal sounded.

"People, there's a foul stench surrounding all this," said Carl Pappas, the bizz jockey. He inhaled deeply. "Can you smell it too?"

***

Request from the author

Thank you for reading this novel. I hope you enjoyed it and will be willing to write a review on the online platform of your choice. Making that extra effort is greatly appreciated by other readers... and of course by me. Thank you.

I hope you and I stay connected through Twitter, Facebook, Google+, Pinterest or my free email newsletter. I'll make sure you'll stay tuned.

Have a good evening/night/day!

M.H. Vesseur

Twitter @MHVesseur

Facebook www.facebook.com/MHVesseur

Subscribe to M.H. Vesseur's mailing list on www.mhvesseur.com

About the author

M.H. Vesseur has written many short stories for literary magazines in The Netherlands, Belgium, Canada and the U.S.A. He was awarded for the best debut with his first story. In his radio detective series about Carl Pappas he has now written and published the seven short crime novels *CEO Groupie*, *Die Rich*, *Tax Me If You Can*, *Acid Asset*, *Nosedive*, *Power Play* and *Blood Border*. The radio detective's producer Hitomi Sakamoto now stars in her own series, which begins with *North*. M.H. Vesseur also published the novel *Lemniscate*, a collection of literary short stories called *Allusions* and his outlook on the super economy *Burning Neil Armstrong*. M.H. Vesseur is an awarded advertising copywriter. He lives in the forests of The Netherlands.

www.mhvesseur.com

Novels and ebooks by M.H. Vesseur

More information on:
www.mhvesseur.com/publications

Allusions (short story collection)
North (The Hitomi Files: 1)
Blood Border (a Radio Detective novel)
Power Play (a Radio Detective novel)
Nosedive (a Radio Detective novel)
Acid Asset (a Radio Detective novel)
Tax Me If You Can (a Radio Detective novel)
Die Rich (a Radio Detective novel)
CEO Groupie (a Radio Detective novel)
Beloved Stalker
Babyface Junkie
In Snuff Park
Sketches Of A Worldwide Christo And Jeanne-Claude
Narcissist Guru
Territory Game

Short stories by M.H. Vesseur

ALLUSIONS

Glimpses of tomorrow await you in this collection. The ultimate amusement park will offer you death. Everlasting youth will take you to the point of no return. The artificial landscape will fill you with joy if it doesn't scare the living daylights out of you. The Narcissist Guru will show you your many selves. There is the ultimate work of art that will change the planet and the old vaudeville star who is still being stalked. And finally, the coming of the super economy will haunt your dreams. This collection contains the short stories • In Snuff Park • Babyface Junkie • Narcissist Guru • Sketches of a Worldwide Christo and Jeanne-Claude • Territory Game • Beloved Stalker • Burning Neil Armstrong.

Available in The Hitomi Files by M.H. Vesseur

NORTH

Man should fear only one enemy

The only enemy who has the capacity to remove all of mankind from the earth, is the virus. Imagine the worst of them all, a true 21st century killer. It lies dormant in the remote laboratory of a pharmaceutical giant whose hopes of making billions off a vaccine somewhere in the future throw a dark shadow ahead. Then Hitomi Sakamoto, the hard boiled radio producer who's on a rough vacation in the wild nature of the north, stumbles upon this dark secret. She is drawn into a final battle between ruthless scientists, a greedy corporation, desperate but dangerous environmental activists, a cold-hearted assassin and... a manmade virus that longs to escape.

Hitomi Sakamoto first appeared in the Radio Detective novels by

M.H. Vesseur. Immediately popular for her iron work ethics and razorsharp tongue, Hitomi outgrew her boss (radio detective Carl Pappas) and now steps out of his shadow, into her very own adventure.

Available in the radio detective series by M.H. Vesseur

DIE RICH - A radio detective novel

Carl Pappas, the bizz jockey, goes on the air again. His radio show "The Boardroom" is both loved and feared by the global business community. He has a sharp eye for business news and the big mouth of a talk radio host. This time around he has some very wealthy guests joining him on his show: two billionaire entrepeneurs and their future successors, who also happen to be their sons. Of course it doesn't take the bizz jockey a very long time to upset some of his guests and his audience — and that same night the bizz jockey finds himself heading into dangerous waters, in the hands of some very angry rich people. His team — producer Hitomi Sakamoto and sound engineer Don Wozniak — is forced to go out and rescue their reckless boss. And then there are the rich kids they have to deal with...

Available in the radio detective series by M.H. Vesseur

TAX ME IF YOU CAN - A radio detective novel

Carl Pappas, the bizz jockey, is cooking up a real shocker: during a live broadcast of his popular business talk radio show "The Boardroom" he plans to reveal secrets about tax dodging practices around the globe. In the middle of the preparations he and his producer Hitomi Sakamoto face unexpected trouble. Who is trying to shut the Bizz Jockey up in this quiet country under the tropical sun? Is it the local military junta? Is it the business community? Or is the sun finally getting to Carl Pappas' head?

Also available in the radio detective series

NOSEDIVE - A radio detective novel

When a large corporation is struck by a cripling strike among its workers and an apparent terrorist attack on its factory, bizz jockey Carl Pappas steps forward to offer his public support. But as he soon finds out, there's more to the picture than meets the eye. Why is the owner hiding in her large mansion? What happened in her youth that is threatening her after all these years? It's a job for the radio detective — and this time around his boss gives an unexpected hand.

Available in the radio detective series by M.H. Vesseur

ACID ASSET - A radio detective novel

Carl Pappas, the bizz jockey, is feeling good about the prospects of environment-friendly plastics he's discussing on his radio show "The Boardroom". But as he soon finds out there's something not right with the company behind it. Can the bizz jockey protect a lonely scientist against the schemes of a large corporation that smells money? Or will he be unable to stop a revolutionary asset from becoming really acidic? Buckle up for a race against arsonists, corporate crime, dogs, bullets and a dangerous industrial zone in the middle of a blizzard, softened only by some real team spirit.

Available in the radio detective series by M.H. Vesseur

POWER PLAY - A radio detective novel

The death of an environmental activist brings bizz jockey and unofficial "radio detective" Carl Pappas to the quiet island of Islasol. Everything seems to be OK with the local National Park and the wind turbine park in the heart of it.

But Carl and his team soon find out you can't take anything on face value. Below the surface of an environment friendly enterprise lies a darker secret. It's time for the radio detective to unravel the local secrets of wind energy, assisted by his producer Hitomi and a new, unlikely ally.

Available in the radio detective series by M.H. Vesseur

BLOOD BORDER - A radio detective novel

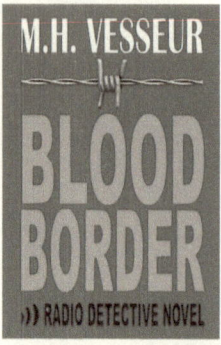

The inhumanity of human trafficking is forcing the radio detective to make a stand. So in the midst of politics and public outrage, Carl Pappas and his team infiltrate the trafficking cartel of a man known as The Clown. But there is nothing funny about it, for the radio detective soon finds himself in the lion's den, a place crowded with former narcotics traffickers and their violent ways. Will they be able to do something about the screaming injustice of immigration or will they become prey themselves?

<<<<>>>>

www.ingramcontent.com/pod-product-compliance
Lightning Source LLC
Chambersburg PA
CBHW030644130626
46552CB00002B/1003